'Moss's ability to conjure up the fleeting and sometimes agonised tenderness of family life is unmatched . . . A great part of a novelist's skill lies in the breadth of their sympathies and their ability to enter into the lives of people unlike themselves. Moss does this so naturally and comprehensively . . . there is an artfulness to her writing so accomplished as to conceal itself.'
Melissa Harrison, *Guardian*

'Moss is a writer who can say more than most others in half the space. Her latest, a haunting story of alienation set on a Scottish campsite, is the summer's most interesting read.'
Independent

'Suffused with fascination . . . this latest display of Moss's imaginative versatility shine[s] with intelligence.'   *The Times*

'This novel – about crisis and isolation in its own ways – moved and encouraged me in difficult times. Another deft, sensitive, crystalline book by Sarah Moss; I loved it.'
Megan Hunter, author of *The End We Start From*

'A masterful and immersive exercise in tension; here are the many conflicting voices of modern Britain in microcosm. Sarah Moss reminds us that society is only ever two short steps away from collapse.'   Benjamin Myers, author of *The Offing*

'For more than a decade, Sarah Moss has been crafting quiet, complex novels that make an indelible impression on the reader. This is one of her best, and most accessible, and should bring her work to a wider audience.' *Irish Times*

'I read this brilliant novel in one greedy gulp. Sarah Moss is an acute observer of modern life and puts humanity on the page with deep understanding and wit.'
Cathy Rentzenbrink, author of *The Last Act of Love*

'Moss has quietly, and it must be said remarkably quickly, been putting out some of the most interesting and carefully sculpted novels of recent years.' *Financial Times*

'Sharp, searching, thoroughly imagined, it is utterly of the moment, placing its anxious human dots against a vast indifferent landscape; with its wit and verve and beautiful organisation it throws much contemporary writing into the shade!' Hilary Mantel, Booker winning author of *Wolf Hall*

'Moss's star is firmly in the ascendant.' *Guardian*

'One of the finest contemporary writers working in Britain today.' *Stylist*

'Suitable summer reading in a pandemic, [*Summerwater*] describes one of the worst summer holidays anyone ever had, in a rain sodden Scottish holiday resort. Cheering in its way.' Margaret Drabble, *TLS* Books of the Year

'This slim and often witty novel brilliantly captures what people think about when they're not thinking about what they're thinking about. The book, told through a series of internal monologues, flits through the minds of a group of rained-on holidaymakers staying next to a Scottish loch . . . But we know something dark is going to happen to this makeshift community.' *The Times*, Best fiction books of the year 2020

'A seductive multi-voiced novel. Some holiday cabins surrounded by pine forest beside a remote Scottish loch grow more claustrophobic and ominous as the days pass and the relentless rain falls on the inhabitants. And then the catastrophe happens . . .' Val McDermid

SUMMERWATER

Sarah Moss is the author of seven novels including *Ghost Wall*, which was longlisted for the Women's Prize, and a memoir of her year living in Iceland. She was born in Glasgow and grew up in the north of England. After moving between Oxford, Canterbury, Reykjavik, West Cornwall and the Midlands, she now lives in Dublin, where she teaches English and creative writing at UCD.

Sᴀʀᴀʜ Mᴏss

SUMMERWATER

PICADOR

First published 2020 by Picador

This edition published 2021 by Picador
an imprint of Pan Macmillan
The Smithson, 6 Briset Street, London EC1M 5NR
EU representative: Macmillan Publishers Ireland Ltd, 1st Floor,
The Liffey Trust Centre, 117–126 Sheriff Street Upper,
Dublin 1, D01 YC43
Associated companies throughout the world
www.panmacmillan.com

ISBN 978-1-5290-3547-6

5 7 9 8 6 4

A CIP catalogue record for this book is available from the British Library.

Typeset in Apollo MT Std by Palimpsest Book Production Ltd, Falkirk, Stirlingshire
Printed and bound by CPI Group (UK) Ltd, Croydon, CR0 4YY

Visit **www.picador.com** to read more about all our books
and to buy them. You will also find features, author interviews and
news of any author events, and you can sign up for e-newsletters
so that you're always first to hear about our new releases.

the sounds of blood and air

Dawn. There's no sunrise, no birdsong.

Light seeps over the water, through the branches. The sky is lying on the loch, filling the trees, heavy in the spaces between the pine needles, settling between blades of grass and mottling the pebbles on the beach. Although there's no distance between cloud and land, nowhere for rain to fall, it is raining; the sounds of water on leaves and bark, on roofs and stones, windows and cars, become as constant as the sounds of blood and air in your own body.

You would notice soon enough, if it stopped.

she could have kept going

JUSTINE HAS SLEPT the way she used to sleep before taking a morning flight. You wake to check the time, reach out in the dark for your phone, for the button you can find in your sleep. It tells you not yet, there are hours still, hours you can spend warm and oblivious, almost as many as when you last looked.

You dream of packing and hurrying, and wake again: it must be nearly time, might even be late, but only twenty minutes have passed. Sleep again, wake again, the short summer night lasting implausible hours, something deep in your brain, some ancient bit of wiring or plumbing originally developed to deal with the beginning of the salmon run or the week the berries ripen, unable to settle. She can't set an alarm because it would wake Steve, but something in her mind – in the part that looks after the breathing and the heart and the listening for the kids while she's asleep – knows the time, reads the tilt of the earth and the turn of the sky.

*

She opens her eyes, looks at the pine panelling not a foot from her face, at the knots in the wood and the bubbles in the varnish rough to the touch, like scabbed skin. There won't be a plane this summer, or next. Who could afford to travel, now? If she'd known, she thinks, if she'd known that she wasn't going to achieve financial comfort or even security as the years went by, if she'd recognised the good times when she had them, she'd have travelled more when she was young, she'd have bought one of those train tickets, those passes, and gone everywhere, northern Norway to Sicily, Istanbul to County Clare. She'd have taken a year out, several years out, before settling for Steve, worked her way round waitressing or whatever. If she'd had the confidence then, if she'd known how to apply for a passport and buy a ticket and board a plane when she was young enough to walk away. She should have gone to Paris and Vienna, to Venice. It's hard to imagine now how she'll ever see vineyards terraced above a sparkling sea, olives ripening silver-leaved or a sunlit orange grove. It probably doesn't matter, really. But she would have liked the kids to hear languages they don't speak, or don't speak yet, to eat food they don't recognise, to cross roads with the cars on the wrong side, see with their own eyes that the world is wide and ways of doing things mostly just habit. Not that you can't still hear

4

languages in Manchester, of course. Not that there aren't strange things to eat. Not that her kids will eat strange things, not that they've shown any interest in languages.

Anyway, here it is, 5 a.m., as planned, daylight already. Time to get out and back and showered before the boys are wanting breakfast. Other people lie in, on holiday, especially after being kept awake half the night by those selfish fuckers with their loud music who must have known they were ruining the sleep and hence the next day for all the little kids and their parents and the old folk and all. Justine didn't much mind, just read on her tablet until she was sleepy enough not to be bothered, and the kids slept right through the way they sleep through the smoke alarm at home – always cheering, that – but Steve got his knickers in a bit of a twist and Justine bets that family with the baby had a bad night, right next door to it as well. They've had parties twice this week, not really a problem you expect out here, away at the end of the road, it's where you come for peace and quiet – anyway, she inches herself to the edge of the bed, not turning or rising or disarranging the duvet in any way that would subject Steve to a draught, not that it ever occurs to him to moderate his own insomniac walrussing to save her rest, coughing and scratching and throwing himself around. He won't even sit down to pee now he's started getting up in the middle of the night, would rather wake her pissing like a horse than sit like a woman just the once. It's a thin partition, she says, I can hear everything, it's not nice. It puts you off, lying there listening to aggressive peeing from someone who could perfectly well just bloody sit down but won't because in his head the masculinity police are watching even in the middle of the night, hiding, peering in through the windows or crouching in the laundry basket. Which is admittedly big enough for a couple of coppers. She has no idea how she'll get all the clothes dry in this weather, not that you come to Scotland expecting sun but this is really a bit much, day after day of it, torrential – all very well the cabin coming with a washing machine but it's actually less hassle to wash things by hand than dry them without a dryer. Getting wet is always the easy part. She rolls neatly to her feet and dips her head while everything blurs and dims and rings and then comes back into focus. Low blood pressure, she'll live for ever. She's learnt the creaks of this floor now, makes a long stride over the worn patch. Steve'll whinge if she wakes him, try to get her to have sex instead of running, easy enough to fend him off but then she's started the day, started the ticking clock of what she ought to be doing, wife and mother, on holiday, cleaning and breakfast and fun for the kids, making memories and making sure to photograph them in case they turn out not to be memorable after all. She sidles where the carpet is unworn. Christ this carpet, what were the owners thinking?

Back-street pub circa 1988, that's what. Even if it's clean, it makes you think they're hiding filth, like the upholstery in a bus.

She floats paper in the loo to muffle the noise, sits forward, doesn't flush. Washes her hands properly, Imperial Leather for a nostalgic holiday treat, always takes her back, used to seem so posh thirty years ago in Libby's house where they also had branded biscuits and real Coke. You're not supposed to put soap on your face at her age, dries the skin and gives you wrinkles, but she likes the tight clean feeling and she doesn't have dry skin or wrinkles. She scoops water into her mouth, the taste different from at home, more like the smell of outside, growing plants and damp earth. Another handful, not that she'll sweat much in the rain but it's easier with more fluids on board.

She left her kit ready in here last night. Yesterday's knickers, they'll be in the wash as soon as she's back; the moment of fear as she fights to get her elbows through her sports bra. One of these days, she thinks, one of these days a woman is going to die doing this, or at least dislocate her shoulder, and it'll be worse getting it off all wet. She probably doesn't need it anyway, the special tight bra, but they always say you must, however tiny your tits, or terrible things will happen. Running socks,

Steve has no idea how expensive but they do make a difference and she's just the one pair, cheap vest top made in Bangladesh doubtless by kids younger than hers but what can you do (not buy it, obviously). The thing about running in the rain is to wear as little as possible, your skin's waterproof and it's layers of wet fabric that make you cold, not to mention the chafing. Capri leggings, she's not shaved her legs, no point in this weather, but any other loon out there in this rain will have better things to think about.

She looks in the mirror. So maybe she was wrong about the wrinkles. So what?

Both hands to ease the door handle, stop at the children's door to unravel two sets of breathing, dither about whether to take the one key leaving them locked in and needing to go through the windows in a fire, the windows being low and easy to open and there being no plausible cause of fire just now, or leave the key meaning that she can't lock the door and there are three beloved souls sleeping undefended in the woods, or at least two beloved souls and one mostly tolerated one. Fire, she thinks, is more likely than murderous nutters, you do hear of psychopaths hanging out in holiday parks but only in America and the good thing about being at the end of a ten-mile single-track road is that the getaway options are crap. Unless, of course, the nutter plans to hide in the woods until dark, but there's not much dark this time of year and wouldn't the police bring dogs? Or he could swim across the loch, at least if he'd thought to bring a wetsuit. Or she. Women can probably be serial killers too, wasn't there one in Japan, though that was life-insurance fraud more than sadism, not that it makes much difference to the victims, though a fraudster probably kills you faster than a sadist so maybe it does. You'd need to get into the wetsuit before embarking on your murderous games, not something you want to be doing between committing a crime and leaving the scene, even worse than putting on a sports bra. Jesus, look at that rain. There's almost no point putting clothes on for that, if she'd brought her swimming costume she'd wear it. One thing, it can't keep up like that all day, there can't be that much water up there. She sits on the veranda to fasten her shoes, to adjust her armband and choose her music. She should probably run mindfully here, listening to the wind in the trees and the lapping of the loch and any birds deranged enough to attempt flight in the deluge but fuck that, she needs music for her feet, music to connect her feet to the ground so she doesn't have to think about it. It's not, she sees, even half-five yet, she can have two hours if she wants them, get in a quick 20k, though if she does that she'll be eating all day and the kids wanting a snack every time they see her but she knows she's going to do it anyway. She's got four peanut protein bars tucked into her packet of sanitary towels in the suitcase, the only place no one else is likely to look, and she's not too proud to eat them in the bathroom if she has to.

And off, feet pattering, heart and lungs surprised, labouring. Cold water on bed-warm skin and why is she doing this again, exactly? The holiday park is asleep, curtains drawn, cars beaded with rain. The log cabins, she thinks again, are a stupid idea, borrowed from America or maybe Scandinavia but anyway somewhere it rains less than Scotland, when did you see wooden buildings anywhere in Britain? Turf, more like, up here, stone if you've got it, won't rot. And they don't look Nordic – not that she's been but she's seen pictures – they look dated, an unappealing muddle of softening wooden walls and cheap plastic windows, the sort of garden shed you'll have to take down sooner rather than later. One thing to rent for a couple of weeks, even if obviously the wrong couple of weeks, weather-wise, but even if you had the means wouldn't it be an admission of defeat to buy one? You've only to look at the woodwork to see that they're depreciating assets anyway, if you've got money you might as well spend it on visas and plane tickets and not pass what are supposed to be the best weeks of the year watching a loch fill with rain. She must check the bank balance, next time there's internet. Steve was right, she'll admit that, camping would have been a mistake, worse than staying at home, but they're not cheap, these chalets, not in the school holidays. She'll be needing to buy new uniforms for the boys when they get back, Noah's ankles poking out of his trousers weeks before the end of last term and she needs to dig out his old plimsolls for Eddie and isn't the car needing its MOT before the end of the month? They can always just not drive it for a couple of weeks till the salaries come in, done that before, her on her bike and Steve on the bus, it's a luxury anyway, really, the car, they should maybe sell it while it's still worth something. She leaps a puddle, feels a cold muscle stretch. She could do anything, this hour of the morning, steal laundry sagging from racks on a couple of verandas – that won't work, she thinks, the air's too damp, they'll have to take it in – nick a boat from the pontoon and go explore the islands, set fire to one of these stupid big cars that will be dry enough underneath, but she won't because she's running now, you don't stop once you've started, not even to set fire to things that need burning down. She'd thought maybe that old couple next door might be stirring, she saw him this time yesterday sitting with his tea and the French windows open onto the rain, they say old people wake early. Maybe he's awake and reading in bed. Maybe he and his wife lie together in the mornings, talking, or even – well, it would be nice to think that might be waiting in the future. After another twenty-five years with Steve. Or not. Goodness knows what they do here all day, that pair, the wife takes ten minutes of shuffling and grasping to get herself into the car, can't be hiking or boating or cycling and what else is there out here? Steve says he talked to the man on his way back from the pub, they bought the cabin brand new thirty years ago and they're thinking of selling now. To a nice local family, he said, said Steve, they just don't get it, do they, that generation, what nice local family does he think has that kind of money to burn? Anyway the old guy says his wife's not up to walking these days and doesn't like to be left on her own so there's not much point, really, any more, you'd be coming to watch the rain, wouldn't you. Gave me the creeps and all, said Steve, he had these kind of sad eyes, never mind that stupid car.

Along the track to the beach where people launch boats, each leaf bouncing under raindrops, slippery mud and the trick is a short gait, don't be on the ground long enough to slip, same as for ice, your feet are for staying airborne, pushing off not landing. Justine's never going to get like the old man's wife, she's going to keep running until she dies. You're not supposed to be judgemental, she knows that, she tells the boys, it's not that anyone's fat or slow by choice, no one gets up one day and decides to eat until they can't move so have some sympathy lads, basic human decency, but you see people sometimes, when you're running fast, dripping sweat, specially old ladies, powder and lipstick to totter to the corner shop with one of those trolleys because they've not bothered to lift anything heavier than a biscuit since the menopause, who give you a dirty look. Unladylike, mesh vest and red face, ought to be at home with her kids. Or those huge women that time in Scarborough, wobbling along the Promenade like milk floats, who shouted at her, *skinny bitch*, and she thought, what you are going to do, hm, chase me, bring it on love, bring it on. You can't help thinking, well, if you'd done a bit more of *this* you wouldn't be like *that*, would you now?

Up the drive towards the road, towards the end of the road, stones hard in soft mud. Round the barrier you have to activate with an electronic fob, as if they, the holiday park owners, anticipate ram-raiders or terrorists with vans. Onto the tarmac, easier. The slugs have come out, the kind with orange flashes, and worms drowned in puddles, swollen white like dead skin. She runs on her toes, nimble around the slimy bodies. Things shouldn't be made like that, unprotected, lying around waiting for sharp beaks and fleet wings, for boots and tyres. Proper creatures run away when you run towards them. No cars, she doesn't even bother listening, turns up the music as her body finds its rhythm. There. Past the pub, up to the big car park at the end of the road under the trees, empty now but for an illegal tent back in the wood near the picnic place. It's been there days, wouldn't you think campers would want either the shower-blocks and kitchen sinks at the waterside campsite or to be off-grid altogether high in the hills? It's a bit odd, isn't it, to lurk here at the very edge of where people stay? And they're sleeping, she thinks, just the other side of the blue fabric, lying there on the ground. Any wetsuit-wearing psychopath would start there, wouldn't he, stoop and slide the zip, peer in, rubber-hooded. She can see where a shoulder pushes against the side of the tent, holding the inner layer in disastrous contact with the outer one. Poor sod. Unless, of course, he is the psychopath. They must sleep somewhere, serial killers, must, in fact, lurk, probably on the edges of where people stay. Oh, stop it, some lad who can't afford the campsite, more like, hasn't she done it herself, once upon a time along the Pennine Way, camping wild and sneaking onto a campsite for a hot shower? Her feet find the track, carry her past the trailhead for the mountain. One of these days she's going to run all the way up there, an easy enough path, but not in the rain, she'd see nothing from the top, and isn't that the point of climbing a mountain, to look down on the people who haven't?

Breathless, not too fast now. There's a feeling like a change of gears that comes after the first ten minutes, as if the engine was labouring and now it's smooth, any minute now it's coming, and meanwhile look at the oaks, the blue depth of them, and the raindrops hanging from pine needles like Christmas decorations, and her top darkening, starting to cling. There's the smell of cold green things, there are fallen needles and pine cones bouncy under her feet. Leap a puddle, easier now, wet feet won't matter later, once they're warm, and here it is, the shift, the running element, like getting into a lake and at first your body says what are you doing, this water is icy, these are boobs, they're meant to be warm, but you keep going, you swim, you push and glide, belly and lungs floating the way they did before you were born and it's not cold, not once you get used to it. It's like that, running, after the first mile. Your body knows how.

*

Round the little headland, the track rougher, stones larger, footwork. She'd be able to see up the valley into the mountains, here, if it weren't for the cloud. There's the old stone barn in the clearing, by the remains of the house; the family must have built the barn better than the house, hundreds of years ago, whenever it was. People used to live all along here, there are the ruins of cottages and byres scattered the length of the path. Farming, she supposes, probably some fishing, but also haphazard little quarries. Whatever it took to get by, just like home, but harder; colder, dirtier, less comfortable. She licks water from the hair dripping onto her face and the vest's dark with wet, maybe she'll just take it off and after all women do run in crop tops, don't they, and she's in as good a shape as any, visible abs in her forties after two kids, but still, a woman of her age, though maybe she should take everything off, the whole lot bar the shoes and the expensive socks, that'd see off any baddies in the trees, a middle-aged woman with an old-fashioned bush maintaining 12k an hour. Well, nearly that, anyway, sometimes. Not that she measures, not that she cares. If Steve doesn't like it, if he's been watching porn and seen the alternatives, he's more sense than to say so. They should again soon, really, never mind the thinness of the bathroom walls, must have been two weeks, three − four? − and even when she doesn't feel like it, it seems to be good for them, like oiling your bike chain, doesn't have to be fun but it stops things falling apart.

The cloud eddies across the trail in front of her. Uphill, careful, loose gravel. Faster, not far to the top now, get some cardio done. Pain flickers in her knee, one of those things, and the mist is thinning, she can see it lying under her running feet, filling the loch and the valley. It's not clear up here, still raining, no blue sky or anything like that, she can't even see the other side of the water but who'd want that view, it's just a stream of cars and lorries and coaches heading for the Highlands, every pair of wellies, every tin of shortbread, every English family who've convinced themselves that the south coast is crowded and expensive and the glory of Scotland's landscape makes up for the weather, squeezing down this one road to be pushed out into the mountains and coasts at the other end, who wants to look at that? That's why she chose the holiday park on this side. You should get a different kind of person here, Justine's kind of person, those who don't need fried food and warm sweet milky drinks always on demand, gift shops and public toilets, people who want to get out of their cars, who aren't scared of weather, whose idea of fun involves using their own two feet to get away from all that. Or at least that's what you'd think; as far as she can see quite a few of the other people don't leave their cabins at all except in their cars, must be spending hours going up and down the road every day, no wonder it's not safe to let the kids ride their bikes.

Flat between the trees, roots veining the path, straight through the puddles now, can't get any wetter. There'll be hikers out soon, the ones walking the whole trail under huge rucksacks and their calves bared to the ticks which isn't clever, not around here, doomed by hostel bookings to finish the day's distance whatever the weather. She could run the whole trail, she thinks, she'd like to do that, but not with one of those bags. She'd like to run from Penzance to John o' Groats, from Paris to Vienna. Well, maybe not over the mountains but you can go round, can't you, up the Danube or something? She could probably handle a few passes, anyway, anything people can cycle Justine can run. She'd like to run from San Francisco to Vancouver, not that she wouldn't miss the kids.

Behind the music, the sounds around her change. A wind strokes the hillside, disturbs the trees, lifts the rain sideways into her face. Go on then, rain on me.

She thinks of the blood pulsing on one side of her skin and rain on the other, the thin membrane so easily opened, of the threads of blood in water. She had a waterbirth with Eddie, felt the baby's waters go into her own pool, Russian dolls of membrane and fluid. Leaves flutter in the wind and rain, the valves of her heart flicker, currents of water move in the loch below her running feet and rain filters through earth where the roots of oak and beech reach deeper, spread wider, than the trees' height. There are waterways through the soil, aren't there, trickles and seeping, and the branching streams within her body, the aortic river and the tributaries flowing from fingers and toes, keeping her going.

Faster, then. Faster. The wind is lifting the mist, making a space for her between the rocky trail and the low sky. Breathing room, steady now. She can feel her core muscles responding, her belly and her backside holding her, letting thighs and calves and the unthought muscles and tendons of ankles and feet stretch and hold, lift off and land. She could go on for ever, easier than turning back, but she must turn, must make breakfast and see that the kids brush their teeth and create the day for them, not yet, a few more minutes, just up there to where the path levels, broadens, where if you could see today she'd be able to see miles, down the loch towards the town and the station and up the Ben with the whole Highlands peering over its shoulder, leaning south. Breathing room, damp and oak and pine and her feet finding their way, rain and sweat in her eyes, she'll remember this later in the year when she's running by orange street light under a brown sky, keeping an eye out for dog poo, she'll remember how she could have kept going.

The track turns and runs back under the trees, rivulets carrying soil and sand towards the loch, patterns of sediment like ripples on a beach. Not much point going down just to turn round and come up again, she could turn here. It's not that she minds hills, not when they happen to be where she's going, but she doesn't go looking for them, doesn't do training, intervals and hill reps, doesn't join the running club, doesn't race against anyone but herself. But you could probably run a marathon, Vicky tells her, Vicky who starts Couch to 5K every six months and gives up because she's too busy or there's weather or she doesn't like being out in the dark. Of course Justine could run a marathon, she does the odd 25-miler just to show that she can and it's not hard, you run and keep running until the end, but she doesn't see why she should, just because some bloke in Ancient Greece was too excited to find a horse or a chariot or whatever people normally used when they wanted to go faster than they could walk. Women run marathons for sure and good luck to them, but it seems to her such a blokey thing, 26 point whatever miles and all that chatter about minutes and seconds and splits and Personal Bests, are we not measured and recorded and found wanting often enough already these days? Why not just run?

*

Oh well, she's down the hill now, may as well keep going a bit, just a few more minutes, they'll probably all still be asleep when she gets back anyway, though maybe Steve in his dressing gown, picking at his feet and doing the cross-word from last weekend's paper which is pointless but harmless – the crossword, not the picking, the picking makes Steve much more likely to have his scratching fingers bashed with some handy domestic implement, with the iron or the big orange pan, than he seems to understand. It doesn't change anything, does it, doing a puzzle, you don't learn anything or make anything. It's exercise for the brain, Steve says, stops you getting dementia, running doesn't change anything either, you have your hobby and I'll have mine. Anyway it's a bit weird, he says, the amount you run, it's not normal, you do know that, you're addicted. Fuck off, she says, yes I do know it's not normal, normal is sitting on the sofa pushing cake into your face and complaining about your weight until you get type-two diabetes and they have to cut your feet off and then you die, no thanks. And she's out and back before the kids are up, isn't she, and if it keeps her fit and well into old age he should be grateful, she knows who'll be looking after whom.

She must turn back. She can hear her children turning in their beds, scent their morning breath, feel on her fingers the roughness of their uncombed hair. There'll be small bare feet on that carpet, small morning erections in dinosaur pyjamas. She'll just go to that bay ahead, where the loch laps boulders and tree-roots under the fog, a tenderness between water and land that's almost a beach, and she'll pause there, a moment's triumph before she turns back.

And she does pause and she does rest, inhales the morning through the rain, is still, lets water drip from her hair and her top. Here she is, under this mountain, beside this loch. Here, now.

She sets off again before her muscles cool, before the body's equations change again, back up the hill, under the trees, along the shore. There is a hiker, and another two, mummified in waterproof coats and trousers and gaiters, their rucksacks wrapped in tarpaulin. Just run, she thinks, take it all off and run, and she's at the top of the hill above the car park when it happens again. Does it feel like a fish in your chest, the doctor said, patients often say it's like a fish flopping. A bit, she'd said, watching him hold the probe on the bones above her breast the way they'd held it on her belly for the babies, thinking more like a bird, really, a flutter, a brush, nothing to worry about, nothing worth bothering the doctor for if she hadn't collapsed at the top of the stairs at work. Turned out to be nothing, she said later, to Steve and to HR and to her mum, after the ambulance and the oxygen and the ECG. Nothing at all, I'd run that morning and not got round to breakfast, I've always been a fainter, remember when I was carrying Noah? No reason to stop running, one funny turn.

It's more than a wingbeat this time, as she splashes through the brown puddle that now covers the whole width of the path. More, she thinks, grinning at the menagerie now imagined in her ribcage, at the entire damn food chain gathered in the chambers of her heart, more like a small mammal, something with hurrying feet. Smaller than a hare. A vole, doctor there's a vole in my upper ventricle. One of these days, she thinks, one of these days, girl, and she pulls off her wet vest, balls it in her hand, picks up the pace, races bare-bellied in the rain past the tent and through the trees and around the barriers at the top of the holiday park, past the bicycles and the blue gas cylinders and the limp laundry and the old man sitting again at his open French windows with a cup of tea. Safety first, the consultant said, there in an overheated pink room with the machines resting between patients, we must think of your kids, they need their mum, don't they, I'm afraid I must say there's to be no more running. And if you really won't take my advice at the very least don't go far, don't push yourself, don't ever run alone.

But what's another person supposed to do, if her heart stops? How would it help, to have a witness?

the days of the first plants

Here is the Highland Boundary Fault, 420 million years ago the dividing line between mountains and plains, when the rocks that are now Scotland lay south of the equator. The sandstone to the south was made by seasonal rivers carrying sand and pebbles down from the mountains in the days of the first plants.

Was that water brown with the sediment, did it foam?

Have the sounds of rivers changed in all those millennia?

What was the riverbed, before the bedrock?

The land under our feet, far under our feet, beneath our buildings, roads, pipes, subway systems, mines and even our fracking; under the valleys, the deepest lakes and the abysses of the ocean floor, is always shifting, forming, changing state. We write on the surface but the surface moves.

Here: to the north, the Dalradian Supergroup, ancient Pre-cambrian metamorphic rock.

To the south, Devonian sedimentary rock, early and late, imprinted by the bodies of primitive plants.

In the beginning was earth and fire. Was there here, then? Was Scotland?

Should the history of bedrock comfort us, in geological time?

the opposite of dancing

ALL THOSE YEARS of getting up and leaving the house before anyone else was awake, David knows how to leave so no one hears. He'd leave his best self haunting its rightful place beside her while his sneaking self, his doctor self, slithered down the stairs and into the kitchen, eased the door shut and didn't turn the radio on – though he'd have liked the news – while he made coffee and toast, read the day's allotted portion of the weekend paper. Earl Grey in the tea-strainer with the dodgy clasp, dash of milk in the china mug with the violets on it he gave her years ago, not too full because the last thing he did before putting on his shoes and jacket, picking up his briefcase and leaving, was to go back upstairs with the tea and say, Mary, Mary love, I'm off, have a good day. It had to do a fair bit of work, that cup of tea: when the kids were small he'd go days without seeing them awake and there weren't always weekends either. Now he makes the tea when she wakes and not before.

*

It's harder in the lodge than at home, to leave her in peace, but he's had enough practice, and if he sometimes suspects she's faking her sleep, just doesn't want to deal with him and the day quite yet, is hoping to pick up her book for a few minutes once he's out of the way, he doesn't say so. Isn't that what he's after too, a stolen hour's solitude? There are moments in his retirement that seem to be the opposite of dancing, a daily game of hide and seek in which the unspeakable objective is to avoid the beloved. He pushes down the plunger on the cafetière – it's not worth having a proper coffee machine here – and carries it and an inelegantly large earthenware mug to the table by his chair. He wrestles with the lock, slides back the French window, lets in the day. It's cold, she'll say, can we shut that door, meaning why did you open it, you know I don't like a draught, but for now he can sit here and feel that he is both indoors and out, breathing wind and weather from a nice velvet armchair with his coffee. He pours, from higher than necessary, admires the shape of the falling liquid and the steam curling from it, an indoor imitation of the mist between the trees. The scent rises, a blend he chose as his favourite after working his way along the shelf in the new deli by the station at home – good sign, that shop opening, property prices holding up – and now buys in small bags, freshly roasted.

You have to expect rain here but not usually like this. Raining stair rods, his dad would have said. There'll be flooding down the road at this rate. It's not Scottish rain, more tropical, not that he's been or ever wanted to go anywhere tropical, insects and parasites, gastroenteritis, Melissa back from that trip exactly as he predicted, sunburnt and underweight and running a mysterious fever. It'll surely ease off later, the weather. It was always the saving grace of being here when the children were young, the one thing you knew about the weather was that it wouldn't last. There'd be a dry patch most days, and if there wasn't, that was what the rain-suits and wellies were for, and in later years the wetsuits and kayaks. His kayak is still under the veranda, resting in the long grass. Might have squirrels nesting in it, but he could get it out if he wanted to, that plastic stuff doesn't rot or corrode, though he hasn't seen the life jackets for years. They probably don't deteriorate either, don't they wash up on beaches years and years later, along with trainers and plastic bottles? He takes another sip, and there's that lass renting what was the Pollocks' place running as if from a bear. Taken her top off, surely she must be cold and really, at her age – he used to have to have a chaperone, sometimes, to examine women wearing more than that, once the Indians started moving out to the suburbs. You'd be surprised, what's often under those burqas and veils and what-have-you, no wonder they get self-conscious. He leans forward to check there really isn't anyone after the lass though he knows she goes jogging most days. He'd not have liked Mary doing that, out on her own at all hours in that Lycra, especially with the things in her ears, wouldn't even know if someone was coming up behind her, and what about her children, who looks after them while she's wearing out her joints, pounding down that hill in her underwear? She looks to be laughing as she runs, not even paying attention to where she is, as if the loch and the hills are no more than a giant gym. The park's not what it used to be when they bought the cabin, doesn't attract the same kind of person. They bought it off-plan, while there were still trees tall in the airspace now occupied by the lodges. You do realise, Mary said, we just spent half your dad's legacy on a drawing of something that doesn't even exist yet? But the old man would have liked it, his son the doctor with a house in Bearsden and a lodge in the Trossachs, kids at the good schools. Still, they should probably have seen what was coming, sold up when Duncan and Maggie left, it wasn't the same after that even while the Pollocks hung on. They did have parties, back in the day, he'll admit that, of course they did. Summer nights, bonfire on the beach, sausages on sticks, a swirl of children up too late and the grown-ups sitting on the shore until dusk became dawn. Hogmanay, even, when there wasn't too much snow to get cars up the road and sometimes when there was, one winter he remembers Mary and the kids getting out and standing under the trees while he gunned that old red Ford up the hill and made it too. But that was different, everyone got together, it wasn't just one lot keeping everyone else up all night and in the early days the music was real, Duncan on his fiddle and there was a piper, wasn't there, could there have been? He's sure he remembers a piper, at least once or twice, hearing it the way it should be, over the water. Even five or ten years ago, you'd never had anything like those Romanians these last two nights, the odd French or German plates on a car in summer but the folk renting knew how to behave. And there weren't all the cyclists and horrible jet skis like amplified mosquitoes and the fell-runners in the skin-tight neon. Not that they didn't use to climb the hills themselves, even must be two years ago now, three maybe, up the Ben when Marcus came for the weekend and there was blazing sun and brave folk swimming all along the shore, but hill-walking's not running, there's time to look and listen. Wild flowers, birdsong, Mary usually knew the names. He could still make it up there, for sure. Well, probably. Who'd want to try, in this weather? More coffee.

He watches the rain. He listens to it running on the roof, to the drumming on the southern windows and the tinkle from the gutter and drainpipe. In Japan, Mary says Melissa told her, there are gardens designed to sing in the rain, with bamboo pipes at different heights over ponds and bronze bells set for raindrops to ring. You could make an orchestra of a Scottish valley, or even a holiday park, set up bells and chimes and drive everyone crazy with it. Next door's gutter is overflowing, dripping onto their metal picnic table. He should have taken care of that, Peter, just because he lets out his cabin all the time doesn't mean someone else is responsible for looking after it. They'd always agreed about that, on the Management Committee, no need to go wasting money on janitors and caretakers and what-have-you, the men were all perfectly capable of looking after their own properties. Well, some more than others. Always better to leave before things go bad, you'd think David would have learnt by now, you'd think those last years at work would have taught him that at least. He and Mary can still go out, anyway, over to the other loch, a nice drive and then a ride on the ferry. It used to be all right to go out for a drive, just to feel the wheels on the road and see the hills rewind in the rear-view mirror, to play the gears fast up the hills and glide down, before everyone had a carbon footprint, or at least before you kept being told about it. It's a good road, up that way. Mary will be awake by now, he thinks, or nearly, and he puts down his empty mug and gets up to make her tea.

Mary makes the breakfast. She doesn't like him to do things in the kitchen, goes round sighing and wiping the surfaces as he uses them, taking the salt out of the cupboard where he's just put it and moving it to the shelf, rearranging the knives when he puts them in the block. They eat muesli, which neither of them likes much and can be hard on the gums but it's good for you and doesn't generate a mess, with fat-free yogurt and lumpy orange juice that tastes remarkably nasty if you forget and drink it after the yogurt. Then Mary stacks the dishwasher and cleans whatever she wants to clean while he takes a crap. He leaves the window open for her, presumably, to do the same, though since he retired it has crossed his mind that Mary appears not to shit at all. He picks up his book while he waits – one thing about retirement, he's reading a lot more – and when at last she appears, face done, lipstick, he asks her if she's still wanting to go out today. Aye, she says, why would we not, we'll be dry on the ferry and it's a nice wee café, I can sit in the warm and sketch. That's what I was thinking, he says, and I'll take my waterproofs, have a bit of a walk.

She takes his arm as she crosses the threshold, and with the other hand he reaches across to hold the umbrella over her head. She's nervous, he knows, about the wet wood, though it's not slippery, and about the three steps down to the gravel. She's worried she'll fall, and that when she falls she won't get up again, and that there will be indignity and pain. Or maybe it's not that precise, maybe she's just worried that 'something will happen' and there'll be no help, no cheery paramedics in green. He conducts her to the car, matching her slow steps, swaps hands with the umbrella while he opens the door for her, swaps back while she grabs his arm to lower herself into the passenger seat and position her handbag cat-like on her lap, shuts the door on her, for her, and goes back to lock up the house. Rain blows under the umbrella. Somehow it matters if she gets wet and not if he does. Just walk, he thinks, this performance of frailty became self-fulfilling months ago. Put some proper boots on your feet and stand on them. They're at the age where you lose what you don't use, even more quickly than what you do.

He shakes raindrops off his coat, gets back into the car. The windows are already steaming up from Mary's warmth and although this car clears the condensation before your eyes, like magic, he leans forward to wipe the windscreen with his sleeve. This is what he doesn't have time for, waiting for a demister, running the engine and not going anywhere. He starts the engine, drives too fast up the gravel track to the barrier. Beside him, Mary sighs, tightens her grip on the handbag.

It's not too far to the café, not as the crow flies. They used to walk it every summer, sometimes more than once a week; nine miles each way but you can take your time, no risk of running out of daylight this time of year. If you walk the trail up the shoreline to the river, the old road takes you through the woods over to the next loch, to the big house on the shore with the converted out-buildings and the jetty. The café is there, in the old boathouse, one wall made of glassed-in arches where once the laird's rowing boats would have bobbed. In the sitting room at home there's a photo of Mary and sixteen-year-old Melissa sun-bleached on the old road, turning back to smile at him – he remembers the tender aftermath of one of those rows between mother and daughter that echoed around that summer like thunderstorms in the mountains, never so far away that you stopped thinking about them – and in one of Mary's photo albums a whole series of the kids messing around on the shore, you could almost say playing, in a way that they had long outgrown everywhere but the lodge.

But those crows don't fly any more, not for Mary. He takes the road fast. Well, he's been driving it thirty years, hasn't he, knows it the way he knows human anatomy. Mary reaches for the handle above the window and hangs on, inhales as if to speak but says nothing. He changes gear, wonders what will be the last knowledge to leave him, will his neural pathways forget their own directions before he loses their map, will the city that's been home all his life swirl and blur while he still holds all those medical-school mnemonics? Will he remember his mother's long-buried face when he can no longer name the Prime Minister? He's still capable of learning, of course. Keeps up with the *BMJ* and he's going to sign up for those Italian lessons this autumn. Might even go to Italy, next summer, if they do sell the cabin, might as well. Hike the vine-yards, Mary could look at art. Oops, bicycle. Rather him than me, in this weather. David, for goodness' sake, says Mary, you nearly hit that poor lad, will you slow down for the love of God.

He accelerates into the next bend, feels the back wheels slide just fractionally as he and she tilt inwards. That's what ABS is for, isn't it, and all the other acronyms for which he paid so much? You couldn't throw this car off the road if you tried. If you won't slow down, she says, you can just pull over right here and let me out, I'll walk back.

She won't.

It's not us I'm worried about, she says, there'll be jog-gers and kids on bikes and all sorts, it won't do, I won't have it.

All right, he says, calm down. He can hear Melissa at the back of his mind, bossy undergraduate Melissa who knew everything and had discovered in her first year of French and Sociology how everyone ought to behave under all circumstances. Don't you *dare* tell me to calm down. They've forgotten, that generation, who gave them equal opportunities legislation, who made space for women in medicine; who treated black and white patients, rich and poor, just the same for the first time ever; who gave women contraception and arranged abortions the first day they were legal. There are worse things, sunshine, than being told to calm down when you're getting into a tizzy.

The windscreen wipers, which detect the density of rainfall and set themselves accordingly, slow their beat. He indicates, takes the switchback turn for the hairpin bends up the hill, a fine smooth EU-funded miracle of engineering that sees maybe two dozen cars a day, off season. How could the English be so stupid, he thinks again pointlessly, how could they not see the ring of yellow stars on every new road and hospital and upgraded railway and city centre regeneration of the last thirty years?

They're in plenty of time for the first ferry of the day, and not many cars in the potholed car park. This water is choppier than theirs, ruffled by a wilder wind, and the valley's cloud is higher though of course still raining. Rings spread in the puddles and he has to pass a few parking spaces to find one where Mary won't worry about getting her feet wet. He wonders where the weather would have changed if they'd walked over, if they'd been out in it, if he'd been feeling the rain against his face and enjoying the protection of his good waterproofs. Well, he'll get out a bit, while she's in the café. He'll go along the shore where the kids once competed to build the tallest piles of stones and dared each other deeper into unnaturally cold water.

The car detects darkness so all the inside lights come on as he turns off the engine. But it is, he thinks as he gets out, raining less. He stands to tie his laces, bends down with straight knees, feels the stretch in his hamstrings.

He holds the umbrella over her, as if he were the door-man in one of those hotels, as he helps her out of the car, waits for her to stabilise before he closes the door and bleeps the locks. She had a phase of locking the keys in her little car, once. Almost every week he'd come home and have to jemmy the side window with the straight-ened-out wire coat-hanger he'd started keeping on hand in the garage. It occurred to him only recently, only after all the CPD courses started blethering about post-natal depression, that Marcus was a baby and Melissa a toddler that winter and in that situation he saw enough mothers too tired to think straight if not actually depressed. Unin-tentional overdoses, silly domestic accidents, the diseases of exhaustion and suppressed immunity. It's not that he chose to work those hours. That's just what it was like, then, if you were a doctor. He saved lives, didn't he? People came to him in their fear and their pain and he made them better, the NHS made them better, over and again without them ever having to think about money. And he gave Mary and the kids a comfortable living, all those school fees and she never had to work, never had to worry, very different from his mum's life. It was what a man was supposed to do and it wasn't easy or fun but he did it, he provided for his family. Look, she says, the sun might almost be going to come out, over there. The sun is not going to come out any time soon. You'd think the sun will never shine again, that it's probably not even up there any more, is drifting away from us in disgust towards another set of planets. He pats her hand where it's holding his arm, gives it a squeeze, and she looks up and smiles.

She wants, of course, to sit downstairs on the ferry and so, to be fair, do the other presumably hardier passengers, including the couple in boots and waterproofs surely planning to walk whatever the weather. David and Mary always used to go on the top, even when there was a gale howling down the valley, and after the first ten minutes the crew told them to go inside, that it wasn't safe for the children. He once caught Marcus spitting over the side, and though he told him off he could see why he'd done it. There's something about fatal drops that makes you want to launch a bit of yourself, just a mouthful, over the edge. I'm going up, he says, only be a few minutes. You'll get soaked to the skin, she says.

He pulls up his hood as he steps over the ledge in the doorway, this boat apparently designed for the high seas, for foaming waves. He wonders how they got it here, before the EU road was built, a steel ship that can carry a hundred souls plying a loch in a valley five hundred metres above sea-level and more to the point four hundred metres above the nearest main road. He climbs the iron steps to the top deck, his hand on the dripping rail warm and dry in his waterproof gloves. Rain spatters his shoulders and his hood. He leans against the railing, feels his bones begin to throb with the ship as the engines churn and the two teen-aged boys in thin jackets with the ship's name across the backs cast off and coil the ropes. He watches the dark water stretch, the grey hillsides and wet trees pull back. This loch is the best place of his life, he thinks, this double retreat, the valley where he comes from his forest lodge for peace and quiet, and he's sorry if that's a cliché, if Dorothy Wordsworth and Sir Walter bloody Scott and Queen Victoria herself felt the same way, but clichés wouldn't be clichés if they weren't true.

He goes back down to Mary after he's wiped rain off his glasses for the third time, and finds her, as expected, chatting, this time to the hiking couple who have spread their OS map across the table. We love it up here, the girl says, one of those English accents evolved to be audible from High Table or the bridge of a battleship or whatever position of command happens to be on hand, and of course the right to roam is fantastic only it would actually be easier if there were public footpaths that were both on the ground and on the map, it's all very well being allowed to walk anywhere but we seem to spend ages trying to find paths. Well, says Mary, don't you have some ad or what-ever they call it on your whatsit, isn't that how people do it now? Come off it, he thinks, she knows what a mobile phone is, he had one back in the 80s, revolutionised being on call. And she does know about apps, what does she think she uses to talk to Melissa? Phone, says the boy, an app on my phone. Yes, well, she says, probably best to carry a compass as well, just in case. The maps come with downloads now, says the boy, and you can sync them with your GPS, but you still can't find a route when it's not on the map. We're hoping there'll have been enough people up there to make a reasonable path. There used to be one, David says, maybe five years ago. I haven't been up since but I doubt it's gone. And if you know where you are on the mountain and there's enough visibility, you don't need paths, that's the point of the right to roam, you can use your common sense and read the land. Mary gives him a look. Oh well, says the boy, we'll do our best, and if it works we'll maybe see you on the way back, have a good day yourselves.

There was no need, Mary says, for that, didn't we get lost often enough ourselves, back in the day? He stands up to watch through the steamed-up windows the vague shapes of pier, buildings, the boys rushing about again. Footsteps run along the deck overhead and the engines lurch and roar. They used to be waiting on deck at this moment, ready to jump onto the jetty the moment the chain was lifted. Aye, he says, maybe we did, but I never blamed Holyrood for it, they could stay in England with their public footpaths and their nasty little government if they don't like it up here, couldn't they? Oh shush, she says, help me up those stairs.

He needs the boys' help to get her over the step between the boat and the pontoon. He can feel her tense as they approach it and she freezes in the gap in the railings, seeing herself fall, catch her foot in the space between the moving deck and the wet logs of the jetty, or confide herself to the wood and find it slippery underfoot, sprawl broken under the gaze of the young men and the couple now consulting their map outside the café. You won't fall, he wants to say, but his saying so will make no difference. I'll hold you, he says instead, and one of the boys says, we'll no let you fall, hen, promise, you just hold on to me now. I can do it, he thinks, she's my wife, but the boy stands with one leg on the boat and the other on the pontoon, swaying a little from the hips with the water's movement, and the other one waits with arms outstretched to receive her. Go on, love, he says, you can do it. She mutters something that he decides not to hear as 'shut up' and takes the step, received by the young man who then escorts her up the pontoon, almost with his arm around her, almost as if she's his granny. David meets the eye of the other boy, who is thinking of offering him help, and steps down without lowering his gaze. Bring it on, laddie, he thinks, just you try.

Mary looks up and smiles as they enter the café. It's one of those indoor spaces that holds more light than the sky outside, its white walls almost luminous, the wooden floor gleaming and the rough grain of the roof beams back-lit.

There's a smell of coffee and wet coats, and a family with a baby in a high chair and two young children gathered around the big table in the window. The children, both in red wellies and muddy trousers, are pressing their noses and sticky fingers on the glass wall, trying to look down into the water at their feet. Smears right across the glass. I'll go over there, Mary says, out of people's way and a nice view to sketch. Will you be staying for a coffee or are you off out right away? Off out, he says, if you don't mind. No, she says, I don't mind, and he sees that she really doesn't mind, or rather that she wants him to go, that she'll probably smile at the sticky kids, let them see her drawing, and strike up a conversation with the mother, who is holding on to her coffee as if it will save her and staring out of the window while the dad reads yesterday's paper. The waitress is busy behind the counter. Will I order your coffee, he asks, on the way out? She'll come over, says Mary, when she's ready, there's no rush, you enjoy your walk.

But he doesn't, really, enjoy it. You don't live your whole life in Scotland to be scared of the rain, but this weather is odd, too much, the rain drilling the ground and churning up mud. Erosion not irrigation. The waterproofs are all right, they work, but his knee hurts a bit and it doesn't wear off and the path is so muddy he decides to go the other way, along the road, not that he's scared of slipping but it's no fun, picking your way through mud,

43

and it's not much more fun walking into a driving rain that settles on his glasses and drips off his nose, and between the glasses and the hood and the cloud he can't see much of the landscape anyway. He should be away at least forty-five minutes, he decides, not to look as if he gave up, and so he walks, hands jammed in pockets, knee aching and pulling, for twenty-three minutes before he turns around. It's a bit easier, or at least a bit less unpleasant, with the wind at his back. He bows his head and keeps going. She'll be surprised to see him back so soon, or maybe, worse, she won't, maybe she knows perfectly well that he's only taking so long to save face, maybe in her mind she can see his every step. He peers up from under the hood. There is the new hotel now, in the Big House. He thinks it has a bar, thinks he's seen the menu on the noticeboard by the jetty. Not that he wants to drink before lunch, but they'll serve coffee, won't they, and it's a reasonable enough thing to do, isn't it, to stop on the way back for a hot drink? They'll have newspapers, probably, and he can sit there and read and drink his coffee like the bloke in the café only without the disapproval of women lapping around his ankles. It's a long time since he went to a bar on his own. There might be an open fire, a day like today.

engines above the clouds

There are highways in the sky. The shortest way between
two points on our spherical planet is an arc, and so trans-
atlantic flights follow the Viking sea road even between
Istanbul or Dubai and Quebec or New York: over the
Baltic, over the top of Scotland, Shetland, Faroe, the curve
of southern Iceland and the arrow of Greenland and then
the ragged edges of Canada. Some of the airborne people
close their blinds against the sunlight, settle to doze their
way across the Atlantic. Others crane to see outlines of
treasured places once or never visited, names that conjure
out of past violence exile and longing, glens and islands
from which southern landlords drove the ancestors and
burnt the houses behind them. There was no one looking
from the sky then, no one to see smoke staining the clouds
and a silence beginning in those places that has not ended
since. Cairngorm, Glencoe, Loch Linnhe. Ardnamurchan,
Laig, Rùm and A'Chill. South Uist.

If the winds are right, some people will keep looking,

watching the windows at their sides as others watch the screens before them, reading the map on the water below. If the clouds are right, some people – children, mostly – will look up from the shore of the loch, tilt back their heads as the planes cross their sky, and imagine departures and arrivals. They will follow the passengers from the Old World to the New, imagine other children bound for sun-seared roads towards flat horizons, for prairies and big skies. Not today. Today you can hear engines above the clouds, in a blue and sunlit place, but down here the sky ends at the treetops.

Zanzibar

THEY ARE TRYING to have simultaneous orgasms.

If we can learn how to do it, Josh says, we'll be like a hundred times more likely not to get divorced. I read about it.

Milly stops trying for a moment. Read about it where, she says, on the internet?

He shrugs, as if it's obvious that that's where everyone reads everything, and she sighs. He does read books, she wouldn't be marrying him otherwise, but not the way she does; he likes wartime history and spy thrillers but takes so long to read them he can't be that thrilled. Not that it's not a plausible idea, the sex. She supposes she can see why you'd be less likely to leave someone with whom you have simultaneous orgasms. Coming at the same time suggests a perfect symmetry of desire. A simultaneous orgasm means that neither participant is trying not to judge the other's facial expressions and thinking, for example, about bacon sandwiches to pass the time. Milly's not sure she

47

fancies that. They might be getting married, becoming one in the eyes of the state until death do them part, but she can still get off on her own, can't she? She's still a separate person. She closes her eyes and thinks about Don Draper, an old fantasy but a good one. Well, she was at an impressionable age, still has the box set on DVD it was that long ago, not that she's actually watched it for ages, not that she even has a DVD player, but some characters, some scenes, just become part of your own world when you're that young. She rather likes that scene in season two or three where he seems to be – well, forcing himself, his hand, on the woman in the floofy dress in the hotel corridor, though maybe the woman likes it, after all she has been sleeping with him, and though she doesn't exactly give consent on this occasion she's not objecting either and you can't expect, can you, that couples in the Fifties in sharp suits and big dresses would stand in hotel corridors having conversations about consent before a married man puts his arm around a woman married to another man, leans her back against the wall and thrusts his other hand up under her big red skirt. Was it red? Probably. And Don Draper would know what to do with his hand, wouldn't he— Gently, she says to Josh, meaning the thing has a hood for a reason, stop mashing it as if you're shooting something on a screen, and while we're on the subject, about a centimetre higher would be nice. Well, nicer. She read – in a book, in fact a book about maintaining sex in

long-term relationships that sh
proposed – that it's OK for a fen
tasy because the whole point of
person doing the fantasising is in co
sor and victim, and anyway no one e
being given a black eye or a split lip,
violence against women so much as about a partner who
knows what you want without you having to take responsibility for telling him, and also rape culture limits our
imaginations which means it's not really Milly's fault if her
fantasies are a bit retro. Women, the book said, should
learn to be responsible for their own sexual pleasure and
to communicate their desires straightforwardly; Milly
wondered if the writer had thought about the extent to
which responsibility and straightforwardness might be
sexy. Or not. And she wants Josh to do things she hasn't
even thought of yet, isn't that the whole point of having
sex with someone else, let him make up what comes next
for once, not have to be writing, directing and producing
Don Draper and trying not to think about if there's
enough bread for sandwiches while simultaneously trying
to have a simultaneous orgasm? Not to mention she's willing to bet that someone somewhere does fantasise about
having a black eye, if there's one thing we've learnt from
the internet it's that however unlikely or stupid or downright dangerous the idea there will be someone and
probably a community of someones out there who get off

long-term relationships that she picked up just after Josh proposed – that it's OK for a feminist to have a rape fantasy because the whole point of a fantasy is that the person doing the fantasising is in control, is both aggressor and victim, and anyway no one ever fantasises about being given a black eye or a split lip, so it's not about violence against women so much as about a partner who knows what you want without you having to take responsibility for telling him, and also rape culture limits our imaginations which means it's not really Milly's fault if her fantasies are a bit retro. Women, the book said, should learn to be responsible for their own sexual pleasure and to communicate their desires straightforwardly; Milly wondered if the writer had thought about the extent to which responsibility and straightforwardness might be sexy. Or not. And she wants Josh to do things she hasn't even thought of yet, isn't that the whole point of having sex with someone else, let him make up what comes next for once, not have to be writing, directing and producing Don Draper and trying not to think about if there's enough bread for sandwiches while simultaneously trying to have a simultaneous orgasm? Not to mention she's willing to bet that someone somewhere does fantasise about having a black eye, if there's one thing we've learnt from the internet it's that however unlikely or stupid or downright dangerous the idea there will be someone and probably a community of someones out there who get off on it. And she does earn more than him, and he does the cleaning and she takes the bins out, so isn't she allowed to think about Don Draper and the big red dress? What do you want, Josh whispers in her ear, tell me what you want.

She opens her eyes, considers the tartan curtains and pine walls, the smell of air freshener that she sometimes stops noticing. A cup of tea and a bacon bap, she thinks, would be excellent, but she says kiss me and reaches up to hold the headboard behind her head, which turns out to be slightly sticky. Probably just the effect of damp on varnish but this is – no, don't think that – this is his parents' lodge. Don Draper. The one where he ties her up. Well, there isn't one where he ties her up but there could be, easily enough. A hotel room, one of those silk negligées but him still in his suit. The suit, she suspects, is a lot of the appeal, and what with all the drink and drugs and steak dinners it kind of tests your suspension of disbelief when he takes his top off and he's ripped. He could tie her up with the tie. Josh is kissing her but he's working on her hip, which is ticklish, and ignoring the breasts she's pushing forwards. She should do something to him. She sits up and strokes his head, which means her legs open and his mouth moves around her thigh. They've already tried that and it didn't work and she really doesn't want to try it again, though you have to give him credit for effort. She pushes his shoulders to bring him back to sitting, face to face, and then she wraps her arms around him for a hug, which is more or less genuine. She likes the smell of his neck. She likes the muscles of his upper arms. She likes his bum and his dick and all of him, Milly likes Josh fine, it's just that she's hungry and it's pretty cold when they're not under the duvet and she'd kill for a cup of tea.

He bites her neck and she sighs, which he seems to take as a sign of pleasure. There should be flags you can raise, she thinks, like the naval signals her brother still had to learn even though they must have about a million high-tech ways of communicating between ships. Or maybe not, these days, maybe having sold all the weapons for the aerial bombardment of faraway children's hospitals the nation is in fact protected by people waving flags and dispatching pigeons. Toby used to ask Milly to test him when he was in the cadets. You Are Standing Into Danger; Minesweeper On Active Duty; Man Overboard. Actually That Hurts A Bit; This Isn't Working For Me; Please Get On And Finish Now. Not Tonight, Josephine. I Have A Book I'd Rather Be Reading. I'm Too Full Of Dinner. Though the book doesn't agree, Milly reckons there are things best left unsaid in a long-term relationship. He's moving down towards her breast, which is more like it. She leans back and makes an encouraging sort of sound, and as he flicks his tongue across her nipple she closes her eyes against the slatted pine ceiling and thinks of her last boyfriend but one who never did any housework and slept with at least two other people while they were together but knew what he was doing in bed, not that he didn't need to given how he behaved everywhere else. He was tall enough to pin her wrists above her head and at the same time kiss her breasts a bit like Josh is doing now only more tongue and less lip, and then he'd run a finger very slowly down her midline, following her cleavage and her belly button, slowing, sometimes making a U-turn and heading back up while she stiffened, waited, caught her breath. Hm, that's nice, what he's doing now. She should do something for him, though, he doesn't like it when she stays passive too long, needs to feel wanted like anyone else, and she can maybe get the duvet back at the same time. Not that it's a nice duvet, polyester filling, makes you sweat, and smells like air freshener but it's probably fabric conditioner, Josh's mum's a sucker for all those cheap smelly things that put more plastic into the oceans and more of what you don't want into the groundwater. Don't be thinking about Josh's mum.

She sits up, sees Josh's eyes widen as she rolls him onto his back. She slides down the bed, pulls the duvet up with her and lies down beside him, her knee hooked over his thigh, her head on his chest where his heartbeat drums in her ear, her hand cupping his other shoulder. It's warm and he smells good. Love you, she says, which is true and also something of a negotiating position: if I love you enough, maybe we don't need to have a simultaneous orgasm, or at least not this morning. You're gorgeous, he says, love you too, and he strokes the back of her neck where the hair is still buzz-cut from last week's new style, and runs his hand down the bumps of her spine so she can almost hear wheels over cobbles. What time is it, she says. It doesn't matter, he says, we're on holiday, we don't have to do anything we don't feel like. I'm a bit hungry, she's about to say, but he says, I want to remember this when I'm back in the office, I want to make you come again, we've got all day. She turns her head to kiss his chest. It's not fair to be thinking of Will the Wanker, she wouldn't like it if he was thinking about Shelley, so she tries Don Draper again.

Oh, Josh has gone soft, which isn't surprising, with her lying around like this. And she doesn't like the feel of it soft, you realise there's no bone, so to speak, just a defenceless – well, not a slug, nicer than that, but some hairless new-born mouse or rabbit, something that really shouldn't be out on its own, if she can't sort that out she's going to go make them both some breakfast, though as she gets to work on it – under the duvet – it occurs to her that when she has sorted it out she will have to follow through, they will be back to Project Simultaneous Orgasm. Wouldn't it be totally worth it, he says, just to know that we can do this thing that most couples can't, for the rest of our lives we'll be able to look at pretty much anyone and be really smug. Shut up, she says, sorting it out down there with the smell of fabric conditioner and sex which is probably highly erotic for some, it's not the fucking Olympics. I want to watch, he says, I want to see you, and he flips the duvet right off onto the floor. She sucks her stomach in but there's not much you can do at this angle, gravity being what it is. Bloody hell it's cold for August. One day, she thinks, sorting it out rather more briskly, one day maybe we'll be able to go to a Greek island. No, to one of those tropical islands, Mauritius or whatever. The Seychelles. Or Zanzibar, she always liked the sound of that word. Zanzibar. Oh God, Josh says, stop it, babe, not yet, come here, come back up here.

She lies on her back, opens her knees and cranes her head to see him, to see his face as he kneels between her thighs. He holds her gaze as he – oh, she says, ah, and she tugs a pillow – his pillow, she's not stupid – under her hips and lifts her legs. It's pleasant, she likes to see him too, eyes closed, concentrating. Pelvic floor, she thinks, clenches, and his eyes open and he closes them again as he smiles. OK, she thinks, now then, Zanzibar, we're in a cabin with one of those wooden ceiling fans and a low bed with really crisp white linen sheets on a teak floor and there are French windows open onto a white beach with palm trees and bright water and he's tied my wrists to the bed. Oh god but it's colonial though, isn't it, that one, she shouldn't be objectifying the places that were red on the map. Gender-based domination is one thing, at least for women, in the privacy of your own head, but the whole Orientalism business is not on. Not that Zanzibar's in the Orient, obviously, but she knows what she means. Object-ification, though how you can have a fantasy without – still, it doesn't have to have geopolitical implications, does it? Transpose it to the Mediterranean, then. Greece. She went to Greece, once, years ago, same colour scheme as imagi-nary Zanzibar. Olive trees, sun-bleached marble ruins, a whitewashed house with blue balcony doors open onto sea and sky, scarlet geraniums in terracotta pots. If it's OK to have a sexual fantasy about a country whose economy collapsed. Not to mention the refugees on the beaches, who will end up in the terrible camps. Like the ones on the American border, she did give money for that, but it's not money that's needed, is it, it's voting, a whole lot of voting and there's bugger all she can do there. How can anyone— Let's try a different position, Josh says, come to the edge of the bed, it's higher than at home.

She wriggles obediently. No point in thinking about those children, not just now, it doesn't do any good, think-ing, but she can't help imagining if it was her class, the little P1s last year, could barely cope without their mums for a school day. How can anyone – well, people do, don't they, given the chance, just think about the Holocaust. Well, not now don't think about the Holocaust, obviously this is not the moment for thinking about the Holocaust.

Or any other atrocity, European genocide isn't more important than anyone else's. The Middle Passage. The Cultural Revolution. The Khmer Rouge. Oh dear. Is that good, he says, and she says, mm, which is probably true, or would be if she wasn't thinking about – Don Draper. No, Josh. Why don't we try thinking about Josh for once, with him actually being here and all. If we're into islands, how about trying Barra where they're planning to live after the wedding? Let's have, hmm, a Scandi-style new-build or old stone, the ones with flagged floors and whitewash? There are a fair few abandoned croft houses, roofs fallen in and grass growing through rusting iron bedframes, crying out for rescue, though Josh says they all belong to someone and people can be funny about selling and anyway you have to do actual crofting which wouldn't be her scene. A wood-burning stove only there aren't many trees on Barra and anyway those stoves are terrible for the environment, though you'd think with the wind there the particulates are going to be halfway to Greenland before they get anywhere near your lungs. Not that Greenland needs any more pollution either, the polar bears – anyway, the here and now. A little being in the moment, hmm, you can't expect a man to give you an orgasm if you keep thinking about particulates and genocides. Josh likes this position because he has a good view, which makes her want to perform a little, though with her legs in the air like this she doesn't have much purchase.

No, she promised herself when they got engaged that she would never fake again. What kind of basis is that for a lifetime together, lying about the one thing she'll never do with anyone else? (Never again, not in her whole life, not if she lives to be a hundred? Well, things happen, don't they, not things you plan, who's to say?) This does feel good, it wouldn't be entirely fake, just a little emphasised. Surely you can't expect to get through what could easily be sixty years – sixty years! – without the odd bit of emphasis, a little storytelling. Mm, she says, ah, but she's getting cold again and she feels a bit silly laid out like this. No, hold me, she says, let's try like this, and they move around again. She touches his face, his eyebrow's arch and the plane of his cheek. His lips kiss her fingers as they pass.

Right, then. OK. So there's a tall, slim man in a well-cut black suit. Linen, since it's a summer's day in – in Italy. Bit fascist, Italy. Oh shut up. White cuffs with cufflinks and tanned wrists and she's watching his hands on the steering wheel as he drives his posh car up the loops of the mountain road towards his house, and he's driving fast and he's locked the doors so she couldn't get out even if she wanted to and he's telling her exactly what he's going to do to her when they arrive, how she's going to go into the villa and up the curving staircase to his bedroom which has a balcony looking over the terraced hillside and down towards the terracotta roofs of the village and she's

going to take off everything except her underwear and –
almost, now, try not to be trying – he expects to find her
on the silk sheets, white silk— oh, she hears herself
saying, yes. More. Yes. Oh, oh, there. And Josh, ah, he
says, ah yes, yes.

Ha, he says, so we did it, yes? Mmhm, she says, still
enjoying the aftershocks. She rearranges herself a little. It
probably doesn't really count as thinking about another
man if he doesn't have a face and you haven't got as far as
the décor of his bedroom, let alone taken his clothes off.
It's just a suit, really, a car and maybe a little architecture,
and even the car is mostly a steering wheel and gear lever,
she couldn't name the make or anything like that. I knew
we could, says Josh, we'll have to keep practising. Mm,
she says, well, there's plenty of time. She kisses his shoulder and lies there a moment, feeling things buzz and
contract. Do you fancy a bacon bap then, she says. In a
minute, he says, but she's pulling tissues from the box,
getting up. He watches her, hands behind his head. You're
gorgeous, he says, as she pulls her belly in.

Rain pelts the patterned glass of the bathroom window
and it's chilly in here. She pees, washes her hands and
face, pulls her pyjamas back on. She'll shower once she's
eaten. Her feet are getting cold. The main room's not much
warmer, and she can see rain dripping from the roof onto
the wooden deck, needling the puddles in the gravel,
bouncing the leaves of the big oak. Beyond the trees, the

water lies flat and dull. They'll need to do something soon, get out somewhere, go see something. Even if it's just driving back to the town for the supermarket, she wants to get away from the huddle of chalets, from the eyes at every window and this view of the loch curtained by wet leaves, where she's begun to find herself watching out for the tourist steamer to pass three times a day. She fills the kettle and puts it on, Josh's mum's white plastic kettle. She's going to put a nice chrome one on the wedding list, and a toaster that will take bagels without her having to squash them flat. If they're moving to the island it's worth making sure they have things that will last, you can't nip out and replace a dud kettle there the way you can at home. It's better for the environment that way, people learn to mend things and make do but honestly that might take her a while and you'd want to start off with stuff that won't break. A really good vacuum cleaner, she thinks, and we'll save up for a proper German washing machine, you probably can't put that on a wedding list. There are four white baps left, couple of days out of date but it won't matter with the bacon and sauce and it's a reason to go back to the Co-op. Goodness but it's icy in here, look at the kettle's steam, she needs to get Josh to put the heating on. Don't if you can help it, his mum said, evenings only, we try to do, the cabin's not well insulated, costs a mint if you're not careful. It can't be more than fifteen degrees in here. She pulls her big wool scarf from the sleeve of her coat hanging by the door, still damp from yesterday, wraps and tucks it so the ends don't get in the bacon, sets the flaking non-stick frying pan to heat on the electric ring, turns on the grill with a vague idea about toasting the baps but really for the heat.

There's nothing happening out front. Rain, the loch, the trees, more rain. Ostentatious rain. Pissing it down. You'd think it couldn't keep up like this, that the water would run out. She holds her hand over the pan but it's barely warm, those old electric rings take for ever. Voices out there, car doors; she leans over the sink to see the family from the lodge behind going out, or at least trying to; the dad's sitting in the car watching the rain while the mum's trying to get one of the little boys to put his coat on and the other one's peering round the door. Justine, that's her name. Northern accent, somewhere near Manchester, said this is the first time they've been here and honestly probably the last, no way it's worth the money, and Milly didn't say Josh's parents were letting them stay for free. The child in the coat is now jumping up the steps to the front door one at a time and Justine's gone back inside, presumably to find the other one, while her husband hasn't moved. They must be going somewhere the little boys don't much fancy, though there's one of those indoor adventure places over towards Stirling, she's seen the leaflets, probably full of hectic kids and parents wishing they'd saved their money and stayed at home but still, better for the boys than being stuck in the cabin. Here's Justine, pulling the big one by the arm, and the jumping child sees his chance and dashes back inside.

Milly shakes her head, puts a couple of teabags from the tartan caddy into the teapot, pours the water, watches steam roll and plume. The pan's beginning to warm up, another minute or two. The old couple next door have found somewhere to go too, their car's gone. Unless someone came in the night and nicked their shiny boomermobile. She chatted to him the day they arrived, when he came to put the rubbish out while she and Josh were unpacking the car, of course he knew Josh's parents and the people they bought the cabin from when Josh was a kid. Doctor, final-salary pension scheme, the whole works, probably bought some fabulous Victorian pile in Bearsden for tuppence ha'penny in the Seventies, probably they've got a gîte in Provence or Tuscany or whatever as well though really in that case she supposes they wouldn't be here. Barra's not, it turns out, going to be entirely a refuge from all that, plenty of second homes and upper-middle-class English people of a certain age at play in their weirdly Puritan ways, weaving their own kaftans and foraging seaweed that they sling in the backs of their enormous SUVs, but they don't, Josh says, stick around much past September. Weather a couple of winters and we'll start to fit in. Good practice, then, anyway, this holiday, though on the island there'll be things to do, work, community events. Joining in, that's what they're after, a collective, a way of life that recognises people's dependence on each other and the land. She just hopes it turns out to be worth leaving all her friends. People will visit, won't they? Justine's bringing – *dragging* wouldn't be quite fair but you can see she's losing her temper – the second child out and the dad's got the engine going and the wheels turning almost before the doors are closed. Can't wait to get out of here, apparently. That's it then, she thinks, the morning's drama. Josh has probably gone back to sleep, which means that if she wanted to she could eat three of the baps herself, and if she takes him the last one on a tray with a bowl of cereal as well and a big mug of tea – well, he likes cereal, no need to say how many baps there were in the first place. It's a pretty benign kind of faking.

always wolves

She steps out of the trees above the shore, nervous, ears cocked, her fawn a few paces back. The trees behind them shiver in the wind, cast off rain. In her mind there are always wolves, day and night, a pack of them slinking on the edge of scent and sound. They creep nearer when she sleeps, when she and the fawn bow their heads to drink, when the trees cluster to make hiding places. The wolves in her mind are fleet on land, fast as pike in water, hungry. They can scent her fawn from their hillside lair, from deep in the forest and they are coming, always coming.

She nibbles some leaves, to show the fawn what to do. They both glance back, into the woods.

a stone falling

IT'S LIGHTENING UP, Mum says, barely raining at all now, you'd better make the most of it and get your boots on, you need the vitamin D. I read about it, most kids in this country have a deficiency and it puts you at risk of all sorts, you need to get at least half an hour's sunlight a day. But I'm busy, Lola says, it's not sunny and the rain doesn't look any different to me. She's colouring in. You weren't busy five minutes ago, Mum says, and there'll be plenty of time to be busy later. You don't want rickets, do you? Or MS like Judith down the road? Come on, Jack, you too, you didn't want to come in from the beach yesterday, you can go back there now. It wasn't raining as much yesterday, Jack says. It's not raining now, says Mum, or barely. Come on, boots and coats the pair of you, you can't just lounge around this room all day, you'll go mad, we'll all go mad. Lola looks up but Jack isn't moving either, just lying on the sofa closing his eyes and trying to touch the tips of his index fingers together from outspread arms.

Mum's started pacing up and down again, French windows to kitchen door and back, twisting her hair up tight round her finger and letting it go, which means that sometime this afternoon she'll probably start crying and apologising for crying and crying some more. Lola won't go mad. She's got a head on her shoulders, Lola, Dad says, take a fair bit to put her off her stride. She allows herself the purple, her second-favourite colour, for the girl's trousers. Come on, says Mum, I mean it, get your boots on, you need to be out in the daylight or you'll be ill, people don't recover, you know, from MS. Jack misses and spreads his arms again. Lola outlines the trousers. Why doesn't Dad have to go out, asks Jack. Dad's doing some work, Mum says, remember? He did go out, sort of.

Dad took his laptop to the pub for the wifi. Might as well catch up, work doesn't stop just because the boss is on holiday, we'll be down another week at the end if I don't keep an eye on things, book in the quotes and that. Mum gave up her work last year, so Dad says she can't say anything about his. It's not easy, running your own business, there's no one else to blame if your cash-flow goes tits up.

Go on, Mum says, boots and coats both of you, and Lola sighs like Mrs Singh at school and puts the lid on her purple pen. Only promise me you won't go on the big swing, Mum says, I don't like that one, and you won't go too near the water, will you? I thought you wanted us to go to the beach, Lola says, you know the beach is near the water, right, but Jack's shaking his head. Lola, he says, please don't. Just don't go in the water, Mum says, and you stay off that swing, and watch out for the stones, they'll be slippy. Yes, Mum, says Jack. Mum doesn't go out enough to know that the stones won't be slippy, it's not that kind of rock, but the wooden steps will be. And Lola, Mum says, come straight back here if your chest feels tight, OK? You can see the next thing she says will be come back in, actually I don't want you out in this weather, you know the rain starts you wheezing, don't want you having an asthma attack when we're all the way out here, and now she's thought about it Lola does want to go out so she pushes her feet into the boots and jumps down the steps, pretends not to hear Mum changing her mind.

It is raining. A lot. You can hear it drumming. Lola feels her chest cramping as she breathes in cold and the smell of trees and earth and rain. She checks in her pocket for her inhaler. At first she thinks there are two in there and then she remembers that one of them is a lighter she found in Mum's handbag, in the lining where Mum keeps the cigarettes they're not supposed to know about. Lola likes lighters, the way you just flick with your thumb and there's a real live flame right there in your hand and you think it will burn you but it doesn't. There's a bit of a wheeze when she breathes out but often when she runs the breathing gets easier so she sets off fast down the path to the shore, hurdles over the boulders in the grass and leaps off the edge of the field to catch the small rope swing. It's always been there, ever since they started coming here when Jack was a baby, and every year Dad comes and tests it before they're allowed down here on their own. At the furthest point, she whoops as if it were a much bigger swing and a much bigger drop than it is, and lands in a heap on the stones. Jack's watching from the grass. Lola gets up as if it doesn't hurt. I can do that, he says. Go on then, she says, but instead he uses the rope as a handhold while his feet slither down the bank.

Lola goes to stand in the water in her wellies. She likes the way your feet can feel the whole loch around them but they're not wet. She looks at the waves patting her ankles and raises her gaze slowly, making a line over the ripples – like chocolate on a biscuit – right out between the islands to the other side, where there's the road and people going places, and then the bottoms of the hills before the cloud cuts them off. Lola and Jack haven't been anywhere for days, not since the beginning of the week. We'll make some trips later, Mum says, we don't want to be driving all the way back down the road before we need to and we've plenty of food. Mum doesn't like the single-track roads, can't see how Dad can know there's nothing coming the other way when you can't see round the bends. Lola balances on one foot and kicks the water with the other, watching the shapes of droplets in the air. Jack's found a stick and is aiming it at the trees and staggering at the recoil.

Wet feet. Oh well, not very wet. She watches the drips bead on her thick socks before they begin to sink in and darken the blue, and then she bends down to dabble her hands. She likes the way it looks as if your fingers bend at a funny angle at the water's surface. In summer – well, it is summer, on sunny days, she means – sometimes there are little brown fish, and if you stand still for long enough they'll come and nibble at your feet and fingers, their mouths so small you're not even sure if you can feel it or not. You have to close your eyes to work out if you'd know they were there if you couldn't see them and it's still hard to tell. Lola likes experimenting with the five senses and what people think is there and what they can be persuaded might be there. It's easy to imagine touch, people are always feeling a little push from what's not there and you only have to mention insects, fleas or midges, to raise bites. Seeing is pretty reliable, though in the dark sometimes you can make people see movements of things that don't exist. Or in the woods, especially near that place where Dad says people were buried. What was that, she says, over there, something moved, did you not see. She can make Jack hear things that aren't there if she talks about them after Dad's said goodnight and shut the door. There's a scratchy noise, she says, like claws, and at first he says he can't hear anything but after a while she can call werewolves and zombies to the window, or even under the bed. His bed. She stands up. Her coat's dipped in the water at the front and she can feel it through her leggings. Smell is pretty easy. Farts, or even gas; she made Mum call the gas board one day, insisting there was a smell until everyone else smelt it too and Mum was going round unplugging everything because she thought the toaster or something might just turn itself on and start a fire. That was pretty funny.

Jack is still busy with woodland warfare, not even looking at the loch. She splashes back to the shore. Dad can make stones skim way across the water, twenty times sometimes, and he's taught her too but she's not that good. She picks one up and throws it as far out as she can, but after a promising swoop it tumbles and lands over where she was standing before. She'd like to watch a stone falling through water. Does it wobble and glide, like paper in air? One day she will go diving, will take the seals' eye view of wavering plants and sleeping fish. She's seen people diving from boats and coming up encased like astronauts in helmets and bodysuits. Rain wouldn't matter, for diving. She throws another stone, a more pointed one that goes a bit further. She's not going to go back yet, Mum's probably worrying but then she shouldn't have sent them out, should she, and if she wants them back she'll just have to come out and find them like a normal person.

Though the water on Lola's coat is now soaking her legs.
She shivers, runs unevenly over the stones in her wellies
to the big rope swing, the one Mum doesn't like. Jack's
scared of it too. You have to lean right over the water to
pull it back and then jump from a rock. You fly out over
the loch and if you don't keep it moving after two or three
swings you find yourself dangling over the loch with no
foothold to get airborne again, but Lola can jump and
she's not scared of landing on the rock, nor really of the
water: if she falls in she'll just have to go back to the lodge
and change her clothes, which has happened before and
will happen again, and Mum gets upset about what she
thinks could have happened and Dad thinks it's funny.
She's got guts, Lola, Dad says, no one's going to bully her,
see, Jack?

Lola climbs the rock, hooks the swing with a stick,
grabs the rope as it begins to escape, and takes to the air,
landing neatly with her bum on the branch from which
years of bottoms have worn the bark. She crosses her
ankles and leans back, lets her hair swoop low over the
waves. She's flying over the dark water in the rain, spread
on the air, her feet and her belly and her head passing
through different spaces at the same time. She could keep
going, could follow her trajectory far across the water
before she would tumble and, as she entered the water,
ears and hair slick back, elbows fold, legs fuse, glide and
turn, become a seal, and she would swoop the loch, would

71

rise and eye the cars and lorries storming north, dip and drift to the island. The seals in the zoo have a pool with glass walls and she's watched them swim, like underwater flying, gliding on currents the way a seagull wheels and coasts on the wind. Sometimes she doesn't much want to be a girl, stuck on land. Back over solid ground, Lola takes her weight on her hands, parts her legs to release the branch and drops at just the right moment, lands on her feet like a gymnast after backflips.

There's a girl on the bank, watching.

She's about Lola's age. She doesn't have the right clothes. No such thing as bad weather, Dad says, only bad kit, though Auntie Sue said once that Dad's preferred kit seemed to be a pub and a pint. The girl's wearing shiny shoes with straps and buckles and pink flowers on them, white tights and a denim skirt – denim's terrible in the rain, holds water like nobody's business, you can tell who shouldn't be on the hills because they're wearing jeans, and her coat is the sort that darkens in water. Can I have a go, says the girl, and Lola shrugs. It's a free country, Dad would say. Take turns, Lola says, I haven't finished. And my brother might want a go. I saw him, says the girl, in the trees. She comes down to the rock and realises she can't reach the swing. He pretended to shoot me, she says. Lola shrugs again.

The girl casts around and then picks up the stick and pulls in the swing. She jumps onto it well enough, better than Jack, but she clings to the rope and holds herself upright as she flies. Witch on a broomstick, Lola thinks. The girl has black hair and dark eyes. She tucks her feet up under her, makes herself as small as possible. She doesn't like to fly. If you ever got Mum on a swing, she'd probably hold on just like that. The girl swings in over the beach and back out over the water, scrunched up. In again, and Lola feels her face beginning to smile because she knows exactly what's going to happen. This time the swing crosses the water's edge, but only just. Out, back, still a pendulum but now swinging only over the loch. Lola steps up onto a flat rock, for a better view, and folds her arms.

You can see the girl realising what has happened. Her shoulders clench. She becomes even smaller. She wouldn't, in Lola's view, have had to be especially bright to see that a swing hanging over the water before you get on it is going to be hanging over the water when it stops. I can't get down, she calls. Lola nods, although the girl, twisting on her rope, can't see her. I can't get down, she shouts again.

Lola glances round. Jack is standing in front of the trees, watching, his weapon held now across his body, as they've seen the police sometimes in city centres and at train stations nurse their machine-guns.

Can you help me, shouts the girl.

Lola can, of course. Easily.

She thinks she probably won't, this time.

What's your name, Lola asks. The girl twists herself, trying to face Lola, but she has no purchase on the air. Violetta, she says. I'm Violetta.

Violetta, says Lola. Violetta who? The girl says some syllables. Shit-chenko, says Lola, Violetta Shit-chenko? Shevchenko, says the girl, Shevchenko.

She spins the other way, drooping now, her feet hanging down over the water. Her hood has slipped off her head and the black hair is beginning to smear her face, to drip from its points. The front of the denim skirt, hitched up around Violetta's thighs, is dark with rain.

Please would you pull the swing in, she says. Maybe, Lola says, in a bit. Where are you from? Glasgow, says the girl, aren't you?

Lola looks at Jack, tips her head, and for once he gets the message and raises his gun, takes aim. It's none of your business where I'm from, Lola says, I'm asking the questions here. So, where you really from, Violetta Shit-chenko? Somewhere people scream and yell like baboons all night and keep everyone awake with their so-called music? Somewhere people don't know how to behave? I bet you've never been on a holiday before, have you. We heard you, you know. My dad heard you. He was talking about it. He was thinking – Lola sighs – he was thinking of calling the police, actually. Because it's not fair, is it, one lot of horrible baboons keeping all the babies and old folk awake all night, ruining everyone's holidays.

Lola jumps off the rock and takes a little turn along the beach, ending at the edge of the water near Violetta. So where are you really from, she asks quietly.

Glasgow, says Violetta. Govanhill. You can see she's going to cry, any minute now. She's not even trying to hold it back. I'm getting a bit sick of this, says Lola, I asked you where you're really from. You're supposed to have left, you know, people like you, did you not get the message?

Lola picks up a stone. The water's pretty deep out where you are, Violetta Shit-chenko, she says, and you don't want to know about the pike.

There are hundreds of stones on this beach, just the right sizes, and she doesn't need them to bounce.

beginning to drown

The sky has turned a yellowish shade of grey, the colour of bandages, or thickened skin on old white feet. Rain simmers in puddles. Trees drip. Grass lies low, some of it beginning to drown in pooling water, because even here, even where the aquifers are in constant use and the land-scape carved by the rain for its own purposes, the earth cannot hold so much water in one day.

Under the hedges, in the hollows of tall trees, birds droop and wilt, grounded, waiting. Small creatures in their burrows nose the air and stay hungry.

There will be deaths by morning.

the audacity of small craft

DAD'S DRIPPED SOUP in his beard, and when Becky points it out Dad says he's saving it for a snack later. Alex is going to throw up, he thinks, actual vomiting over the table. His own soup in his stomach bubbles and heaves. What's got into you, says Mum, cheer up, it can't rain much longer. Alex turns away. Look, Mum said, back in May when he said he'd stay at home this year, we're happy to leave you at home for the day but two weeks is too long, not to mention I know perfectly well what you'd get up to, you and your friends in an empty house, not to mention this is our family holiday, of course we want you there. No, you're coming with us. If you wanted to do something else you should have made a proper plan weeks ago. Weeks ago, he was revising for his exams, and by 'proper plan' it turned out Mum meant 'return to the 1990s when there was work for unqualified sixteen-year-olds'.

Nothing, he says. I'm going out in the kayak. Mum looks at the rain rolling down the window. But you'll get soaked, says Becky. Breaking news, he says, kayaker gets wet in Scotland. It's called watersports for a reason, eejit. Don't call your sister an eejit, says Dad. Going out where? Alex shrugs. Round the island, he says, not too far, I can't spend all day stuck in here. You're not stuck, Dad says, leave any time you feel like it, no one's stopping you. Aye, right, says Alex, so that's what I'm saying, I'm going out in the kayak. And no, you're not stopping me, he does not say, and I do feel like it which is why I'm leaving, see? He gets up, takes his bowl to the sink before anyone can tell him to. What about the clearing up, says Becky, why can he just walk away, you're going to tell me to wash up, aren't you? Mum sighs. It's only four bowls and a pan, she says, I'll do it myself rather than have any more arguing. OK, says Becky, fine, you do that, it's not that I mind doing it, I just don't see why Alex gets to go find himself on the loch while I have to scrub pans, it's really sexist. I told you, says Mum, I'll do it.

Alex, heading into the bathroom where his wetsuit is hanging over the bath, reflects that if Becky were really interested in social justice rather than the evasion of chores, she would see that making Mum wash up in no way fucks the patriarchy. Anyway, Dad's the patriarch round here. Or likes to think he is. Alex locks the bathroom door, feels a weight lift from his skull at the sound of a minute's privacy. It was all very well when they were little but it's not decent to make him and Becky share a room, not any more, however many bedrooms the cabin doesn't have. Mum and Dad could sleep on the sofa bed, couldn't they, dress in the bathroom? He considers a quick wank while he has the chance but decides he'd rather just get out there. Away from here.

The rain is pretty horrible, just not as horrible as being in the cabin. He pulls the red kayak out from under the deck and Dad opens the French door to tell him to be careful, not to scrape it on the gravel and make sure he puts that life jacket on. As if he might have had it in mind to wreck the kayak and drown, not that it wouldn't have some appeal given the alternative. How many days left before they can go home? No, best not to think of it. As he lifts the kayak he sees movement in the French windows next door, the little girl and her baby brother with hands pressed against the window, watching him, and now waving as if he were a train and they people standing on a bridge. After a moment, feeling stupid, glancing around to make sure no one else is watching not that you can ever tell on the holiday park, he shifts the kayak and waves back. Train driver. He needs to get out of here. Later, he's going to take his phone down the pub where this year they're willing to pretend they think he's old enough to be in the bar with a glass of Coke and the free wifi and maybe this is the day he'll see if they'll sell him a beer. Cold water runs down his neck. He balances the kayak on his shoulder and carries it over the grass towards the jetty. A gust of wind throws rain in his face. His phone is back at the house, always switched on in case some coincidence of weather and wishing brings a flash of reception, so in his head he composes a post to his group chat and sends it out on the wind. SOS. Mayday.

The wind slaps water around his ears and tugs on the kayak so he stumbles, bangs his shin on one of those stupid rocks people use to stake their claim on the open grass. Fuck, he says. Bloody fucking rock. Assholes. Cunts. Sometimes, alone, he goes on like this for a while, takes out and airs his bad words, but the weather extinguishes his swearing. The Scottish sky is better at obscenity than any human voice. He shifts the kayak, bows his head, remembers the board games in the damp lodge, the smell of soup and the pitch of his sister's voice, and keeps going. He won't die, after all, out here, and he might kill someone if he stays in there. His dad, for example, he might kill his bearded, soup-dribbling dad. Shut up about the soup, he thinks, but its viscous tomato smell seems to hang in his hair. Not blood, he wouldn't want to spill his father's blood, but the satisfaction of approaching from behind with the pan in which his mother fries stinky eggs so the whites are all snotty and slimy and form strings as his father shovels them into his mouth, with that pan or one of these very rocks—

The pebbles on the beach are dark and shiny with rain. He likes their sound under his feet, the proclamation that he is here, real, that he has mass and force and velocity. A child has dropped a shoe on the beach, the wrong kind of shoe, patent black with a pink flower, and if he wasn't carrying this fucking kayak he'd put the shoe somewhere more deliberate, upright at least and further from the waterline, the way people do with found objects, teddies and bobble hats on walls, as if making impromptu shrines. On the way back, maybe.

Right, he can go out along the jetty and launch from there or he can just bloody man up and walk into the loch. Dad might be watching. He walks. It's not a drysuit, you have to let the water in and then let your body heat it around you. It's so cold his feet and ankles read pain rather than temperature. Calves. Knees. Bloody hell. He stops to lower the kayak.

When he was younger he used to pee in his wetsuit, to warm it up.

There are three white birds sitting on the water halfway between the shore and the island. Gulls. Hooked yellow beaks, the black flashes on the heads, bigger than you think, not much bothered by rain.

He's up to his thighs and the kayak is pulling on its rope like an impatient dog. Right then. It would have been easier to get in from the jetty.

Much easier.

Oh fuck.

But it was a slip, not a fall, and now at least the wetsuit

83

is properly full of water and will soon be insulating him the way it's supposed to do. He tries again, and this time ends up more or less in the kayak and more or less the right way up. Go, then, to the island. To the far side. To the end, even, to the town where there's the station and he could, if he had any money, take a train back to the city, if he had his keys go home, though home, he thinks, beginning to paddle, is not where he would go, or at least only briefly for a shower and a change of clothes and to stuff some things into a rucksack. Once you're floating on it, the loch is rougher than it looks from the shore. He finds the rhythm of his paddle, likes as always the percussion of water and body and boat, the audacity of small craft carrying a living soul across a body of water. He'd have no phone, and more to the point no money, but there's not always a guard on the train and if there is you can hide in the loo. He can see a gust of wind coming down the loch, the water ruffling like stroked fur, and shoves the kayak round to face it. He'd go home, and he'd take a hot shower – you'd need one after travelling in a wetsuit – and he'd raid the kitchen, no, he'd put a frozen pizza in the oven before getting in the shower and then, there's no way round this, he'd borrow the credit card Mum keeps in her desk because although she doesn't like credit cards, doesn't like debt, having one gives you a credit history and what if her purse gets nicked while she's out, and he'd go on the internet and find out how you get out of this country because people still do, it can be done — not America, though it's the obvious choice, where people have always gone, but racists and guns and complete fucking nutters, it's not even funny any more, and anyway from what he's heard it's about the hardest place to get through immigration. Australia, red earth and big skies. He's OK at surfing. Windsurfing on calm water, anyway. They have farm jobs, don't they, for young travellers, for Europeans, and they'd stretch a point, wouldn't they, he is Scottish. He could pick fruit, whatever grows there. Mangoes, warm and heavy as breasts. Does it rain enough in Australia for mangoes? Hm, breasts. Or Canada, aren't they nicer than the Americans, couldn't he take kayaks up rivers or something, though that might have been long ago. It wouldn't be worse than here. He knows where the passports are, stupidly in the top of Mum's chest of drawers, along with her jewellery, to make things really easy for burglars. I know, she says, but when I hide things I can't find them and anyway once someone's in your house you probably want them to find what they're looking for and get out, anyway you can't live your whole life anticipating the plans of imaginary burglars, it's not as if we've actually used the passports in years, only for banks and such, yours and Becky's expired anyway. Well, he's only thinking about things, isn't he. There are lakes in Canada, and mountains, he could be there now, could be taking supplies back to the cabin where his girlfriend is waiting for him, his girlfriend with long pale hair and tits like you wouldn't – he's almost past the island and the waves begin to slap the side of the kayak so he can feel each blow. Head to the wind, then, and it'll be really fast coming back. He likes the way you can wander in a kayak on a loch, go over here because you feel like it and then over there to have a look, the activity is 'kayaking' rather than going somewhere and coming back. He could stop on the island, there is even a jetty where the little ferry stops in summer for people who walk around on the trails and read the signs about the birds and animals that mostly aren't there any more, and sit at the picnic tables to eat ham sandwiches and crisps. Not that he wouldn't take a ham sandwich and crisps just now. But he's liking being out here, wants to keep going, maybe even right up to the top of the loch, to where the river comes in off the hills, after all it won't be dark till nearly midnight and it's not as if he has anything else to do today.

He paddles on. The sky rolls, clouds the colours of bruises. He licks his upper lip to find out if his nose is running or if it's just rain, and finds he can lick a surprising proportion of his cheek, sweet to the lip's salt. Let it run. The rain doesn't matter now; insulated in the blood-warmed water of his wetsuit in a kayak on the loch, he has forgotten how it feels to be dry. Drops patter on the boat, wind sings through the heavy air, waves smack the hull and the paddle dips, twists, pulls, drips.

He pushes on, matching muscles against wind and current while on the shore trees lean and toss. To the east, gulls tumble up the sky, wheel and call. Who would choose to huddle in a cabin when you could be out here?

Onwards, wind and rain and running sky, weather pouring overhead down the valley and away south over sodden hills and fields. Alex's shoulders begin to ache, and while the kayak is fine it's true that much more wind would make things difficult. Just a little further, until he's parallel with the tree that looks to rise from the water itself but has in fact twisted its roots into a rocky islet, a tree he climbed a few times when he was younger. He remembers inching out along the branch over the water, knowing there were more rocks biting the surface, that if he fell there would be blood and brokenness and Dad saying I told you so and that these were reasons to keep going. Well and here he is. He doesn't have to do that any more.

He spins the boat, knows exactly when to plant his paddle to point the prow down-wind and down the loch. He is right in the middle, as far from both shores as can be and he would like, he thinks, to be further, he would like a greater expanse. He rests a moment, balances, lets himself and his craft drift. He has been going to school for twelve years, three-quarters of his life gone in the routines of bells rung and queues for nasty food and the feel of nylon trousers, another one to go. It's a lie that Highers are going to be different. Another year. Well, ten months. Jesus. And then what? University, only he's no idea what he'd do there, he's OK at Maths but what do you do with a Maths degree? Then fifty years of work. You shouldn't be thinking about retirement before you've even started, there's something wrong with that and anyway he'll be basically dead by then, sixty-six. If there's still a planet to live on, if the crazy governments have spared anything. He picks up the paddle, but once the kayak's going the right way he's only really steering, dipping and pushing for stability while the water pouring off the northern hills and the wind pushing along the loch carry him back. Hot shower, he thinks, and please God not more of Mum's sloppy brown 'home cooking' for tea. It's not much of a holiday for me, she says, I don't know if you've noticed that there are still meals to cook and toilets to scrub and actually more of it with everyone in the house all the time and no shops to pop to when we run out. And whose choice was that, who the fuck goes on holiday somewhere there isn't even a chippy? It's pretty weird when you think about it, all these middle-class white people coming here to have less privacy, comfort and convenience than they do at home, how's that a holiday? It's a break, Mum says, from what you think you need but you don't really, back to basics, haven't you noticed we're all talking to each other more without our phones? Yeah, he said, arguing more, I had noticed that, aye. And where's everyone else? Alex's friend Amir went to one of those all-inclusive hotels somewhere in like Spain or Turkey or whatever, said there was free food all the time, cooked breakfast and then fruit and biscuits out all morning and then a lunch buffet and ice creams and cake in the afternoons and then dinner, and two swimming pools even though it was right on the beach and loads of hot girls lying around bored on sun-loungers. They had barbecues, he said, in the evenings, chefs in their white hats out on the patio, all the burgers and steaks you could want. It was unbelievable, Amir said, the food and the girls, and a really good gym so Amir had basically spent the whole two weeks working out, surfing, eating and chatting up the girls and barely even saw his parents. Even if you discount at least the more exciting half of what Amir says he did with the girls, which Alex does, *at least* half— he hears the wind coming before it strikes, has time to brace but it's a near thing. Fuck.

Pushing deep into the dark water, driving the kayak on, he sees the gust flying down the loch, battering trees and pummelling the waves.

Fine, he says, be like that, bring it on, motherfucker, and a small voice at the back of his mind asks what the fuck he thinks he's doing, cursing the weather up here, the weather that boils up out of the mountains, over the sea, down from the actual Arctic, is he out of his tiny mind, alone in the middle of one of the biggest lochs in

Scotland, nowhere to hide, you could drown out here, easily. They'd never find your body though the red kayak would wash up sooner or later, upside down, probably, nosing the shore as if it might drag itself out and up to the lodge and meanwhile his body drifting down, down a long way here where the hills slope so steeply into the loch, there's probably hundreds of metres of water below him and pike and all sorts, mostly as far as he knows drowned people fill with gas and rise again but not if the pike have bitten and torn flesh from bone, must be dozens of the dead lying below him and the red kayak, young men running for home before a rising wind, eye on the weather but late, too late. Another gust hits and the kayak twists under him. Dear God, he says, if you let me get off the water safely today I promise I'll never – never, uh – never laugh at Kayleigh Ward again. He doesn't even do it to her face, or not exactly, only when the others are, and if she was all that bothered she'd wear normal clothes, wouldn't she, do something about herself? Right, boat straight again. Those pike will have to wait. His shoulder's really hurting now, tight and achey. He wriggles a bit, can't afford to stop and stretch it properly because only the forward movement is keeping the kayak stable amid increasingly chunky waves. Come off it, he thinks, you're not exactly crossing the Atlantic mate, it's only a loch. Not that you would cross the Atlantic in a kayak. Not that you'd get out of sight of land if you tried, nor probably even off the beach, not in a wind like this. Anyway it's rubbish, the drowning thing, he's got his life jacket, hasn't he, and he's in his wetsuit, won't get hypothermia either, and he can swim, pretty well actually, could probably tow the kayak to land from here if he had to, it's not that far, to those trees over there, and he doesn't have to, does he, he's doing fine, still paddling.

He changes sides again. Ow. Going to be stiff as a corpse tomorrow. Will they let him have a bath, use up all the hot water and shut everyone else out of the bathroom for an hour? He could have a good wank. It's been days, even when he's pretty sure Becky's asleep, some things you just can't with your sister in the room. The rain's heavier, hammering on the hull and he can hear it hissing into the loch as well. He licks water off his face, moves to wipe his nose with the back of his hand but what's the point. There's that tree again, not far now, and some other nutter out there, camo coat but the trees' green is so bright you can still see him, could be a hiker but he's not on the path and keeps stopping. More like just someone else who can't stick being indoors another five minutes, or one of those poor buggers camping, fuck all you can do in a tent all day, wouldn't you just go home? The town at the end is veiled by rain, the world with the red kayak at its centre contracting. But not below, he thinks, that distance stays the same, to the rocks and grabbing weeds at the bottom where the bones lie. Does it make any difference, down there, what the weather's doing? Do the fish even know about wind?

His hands are going numb. Doesn't matter, of course, he can still paddle. But still. Feet too, come to think of it. He'd do better in a drysuit but they wouldn't buy him one, what do you want that for, we just spent all that money on the wetsuit, we've nowhere to keep it and do you think we're made of money? He can get a job, now. A National Insurance number came a few weeks ago and he took it up to his room and looked at it, re-read the letter. How do they know about him, the National Insurance people, how do they know his name and where he lives and when he turns sixteen, have they been watching him all these years? They shouldn't do that. You should be the one who tells them, here I am, I'm ready now, you can count me. Though probably some people never would, would rather skulk in the woods or up the mountains, cooking squirrels and rabbits over a fire – not that you could keep a fire going in this weather, not unless you built it in a cave or whatever and then where does the smoke go – picking berries for the whole three weeks there are berries to pick. He had a book like that when he was little, about a kid in America who ran away and lived in a hollow tree in the Catskills, and though he read it about fifteen times there were bits he could never really imagine, a tree wide enough that you could make a bed and a place to sit and storage inside the trunk, a country big enough that a person, even a child, could live indefinitely without ever seeing another person. He hears the wind, this time, before it hits, but there's not much he can do, the kayak skids under him, tips as it comes side-on to the waves and though he doesn't go in there's fresh cold water in the wetsuit and he starts to shake, a kind of deep shaking that seems to be coming from the depth of him, from his guts or his lungs. Nothing to be done but get home, fast now, and it's true the wind is helping though it doesn't feel like it, this is much quicker than it was going out.

He really can't feel his fingers.

And here's the island, the rowan trees crouching at the water's edge. This is going to be the tricky bit, this turn, no way to avoid crossing the wind, he'll just keep an eye out for another of those gusts. The rain hits his face as he turns, spatters his left eye so he can't keep it open which makes it hard to watch over that shoulder for the wind on the water. Blinking rapidly so he sees the world as if under flashing lights, so his brain can't quite accept the constancy of boat and waves and land, he pushes now fast across the last stretch, sees the old blue rope swing reach in the wind and fall, as if there's an invisible child driving it. Ghost child, why not, you could die there, easy, that was why it used to be exciting, water and rock waiting below instead of that weird rubber stuff they have in playgrounds. Even Mum used to tell them not to play on that swing and normally she was always on about how kids ought to be free-range and better to get bumps and bruises in the fresh air than be inside staring at screens all the time. Quiet fills Alex's ears and he realises that he's had the wind growling in his head, playing in the whorls and drums of his ears, all afternoon. Or whatever it's been, two hours at least, must be, all the way up there. And the waves, of course, have almost gone here in the shelter of the island and the peninsula where even today there are cars glinting wet through the trees, people desperate enough to walk in the rain or some of them just seem to drive to the end of the road and park and sit there, newspapers and tea from a flask and it makes him itch everywhere at once just thinking of it, people sitting in parked cars, the windows steaming up, waiting for minutes to pass, for their lives to drip away. You can't wait for the fucking weather, not here, you'll be dead before it stops raining.

Inside the island, ruffle on the water, the slap of wavelets on the stony beach. He's going for the jetty, this time, climb up the ladder and lead the boat in on a string the easy way, though as he tries to put down the paddle to grab the ladder he finds his fingers have locked on it, the simple matter of letting go of one thing and picking up another no longer works, and he does actually need to get hold of the ladder, or of something. He jams the paddle through the ladder's step, which stops the boat, and then bends forward, bites his index finger and lifts it off the paddle with his teeth, and there's no feeling in the finger but a horrible twang in his forearm, as if a taut string has been plucked when it shouldn't be. Still. He does it again with the middle finger, a lesser twang and now he can hook his arm round the ladder and rest the hand with the paddle in his lap. He blows on it, mouth wide, har, har, until he's a bit dizzy, but then he can use one numb hand to lever the other and they'll probably work well enough for the ladder even if he can't feel them, you probably don't exactly need feeling to operate the body and maybe he'll tie up the boat and come back for it later but he knows what Dad would say. He makes an approximate knot to hold the kayak while he climbs out and fucking hell this is hard, is this what it's like being really old, like his nan, always hobbling and gripping as if the ground's not to be depended on, is this how it feels 'cos if so he doesn't want it, thank you very much, he'll just jump off a cliff when he's seventy or whatever. Drive his car into a wall.

Alex finds himself lying on his belly over the edge of the jetty. He squirms forward, bangs a knee so hard his eyes water but at least the knee still has feeling. He sits up and the shaking starts again. Pushes himself onto all fours and then upright and it fucking hurts, it really does, just standing up really fucking hurts and he shuffles down the jetty thinking they'll be watching him, all those people sitting in their cabins with their loch views, staring into the rain waiting all day for something like this, for a boy making an idiot of himself in full view. Och, Mavis, look, that lad from over the way, can't even walk properly, what's he been doing then. Off the jetty, down to the water, pull the boat up but not too far, don't want it scraping over the stones, not with so much water in it. Tip it, watch the water run out, now lift, come on, pick the bugger up. Jesus. Wasn't this heavy on the way down. Walk, now, everyone's watching, and there's that shoe, she hasn't been back for it, how did the little girl get home without a shoe?

They've put the light on in the cabin and he can see Mum doing that stupid puzzle and Dad fiddling with his phone though there can't be anything new on it. Becky must be in the bedroom or if she's locked herself in the bathroom he's going to break down the door, he has to have a shower. Or a bath. This shaking. His knees hurt as he bends and his arms don't want to move to put the kayak down and his shoulders almost won't push it back under the deck. He'll take the life jacket off inside, when he can unfasten the clips. He shuffles up the stairs, gets the door open and edges himself in. There you are, says Mum, I was beginning to wonder, shut that door love, you're letting all the heat out.

bones of skin coracles

There are few boats. The steamer goes anyway, all weathers, drawing its lines across the water, the captain's amplified commentary rolling over the waves. Here was Bonnie Prince Charlie and there was Mary Queen of Scots and Braveheart and Walter Scott and Rabbie Burns and every Scot you've ever heard of, and if Nessie's not in this particular loch we have our own submerged monsters. The cloud of rowing boats around the village jetty has gone like midges in a high wind, the windsurfers have folded their wings, the jet skis are at rest and even most of the kayakers are aground.

There are other boats, below. There are the bones of skin coracles and the shells of bark canoes and the hollowed-out trunks of trees that once gave shelter to bears. There are the small boats of boys in every century who never came home, and the water holds the hand-stitches of their clothes and the cow-ghosts of their shoes and the amulets that did not help when they were needed.

other silent swimmers

MUMMY, SAYS IZZIE, Mummy, Mummy, look. Mummy? Mummy, look. Mummy?

Yes, says Claire, what is there? She had been wondering how many times Izzie would say 'Mummy' if she didn't reply, but it seems that Izzie can say Mummy more times than Claire can listen to it.

Mummy, look, Mummy. Come over here.

I'm in the middle of cleaning the sink, she wants to say, I'm actually dealing with this brown muck behind the taps that's been bothering me all week. Which is likely to be more interesting, brown muck or anything that can possibly be happening out there in the rain? Claire puts her scourer in the sink − one thing you can say for most holiday cottages, they have an impressive range of cleaning products, none of your eco-friendly fairy-dust − and crosses the room. There is mud on the carpet by the door and two layers of fingerprints and what's probably snot on the French windows, some at Izzie-height and the lower set where Patrick has been edging along and flattening his face against the glass. While Claire's been seeing to the sink, Izzie's been breathing on the window and drawing flowers in the condensation. What if I give you a cloth and the glass-cleaner, Claire says, could you clean this window for me? Izzie shakes her head slowly. Can't reach, she says, look Mummy!

There's a teenage boy carrying a kayak up from the beach, must have been out even in this weather. Though she can imagine it, at that age, how being out on your own in the rain might be preferable to being in a small cabin with your parents. Or even at her age. She does have friends who go on holiday with their parents and she sees how it works, in principle. The grandparents can spend time with the kids and the parents get to go out for lunch together or whatever, but none of the friends seems to have any fun on these holidays. She says her kids never cried, she says in her day you weaned at six weeks and that was that, she says hers were all potty-trained by their first birthdays. Can you believe it, he asked me not to breastfeed at the table? People get on best, in Claire's view, when they're apart at least half the time, and she's not sure that doesn't apply to kids too. It's not exactly that she ever really wants to divorce Jon, or at least not for more than the odd evening every few weeks, but she sometimes envies people who have shared custody arrangements. Wouldn't she be an amazing mother, wouldn't she be patient and creative and selfless, if she had to keep it up for no more than five days in a row? If she had every other weekend to herself, to do whatever she wanted from dawn to dusk, to sleep late and go swimming and get the house properly clean? Can I have a red boat, says Izzie, can I have a red boat to go to the islands? Claire strokes her hair. Maybe when you're older, she says, when you're as big as that boy. Because Izzie will, of course, one day become a person who could take a boat to an island on her own, as old if not as big as that boy.

Claire tries to imagine watching her go. Tries and fails. Wonders if the boy's mother is watching from another cabin, if she's thinking what Claire would be thinking.

Will you clean the window for me now, you can reach, it's only the lower bits that need doing, she says. There's a reason, sweetie, why it's the part you can reach that needs cleaning, she doesn't say. Izzie shakes her head. Make Patrick do it, she says. Patrick can't stand up and hold something at the same time, says Claire, and anyway he's going to sleep, though the last is patently untrue because Patrick is very audibly awake and it's been a good twenty minutes since Jon took him through. It's too early for him to drop his nap, she can't be doing with a fifteen-month-old who doesn't give her a lunch break, and he ought to be tired, all of them kept awake half the night by the Romanians next door and their loud music. Working at the hotel, probably, getting together at the end of a shift. It's not that she minds people having the occasional party, we were all young once – not that the woman who seems to be staying there looks any younger than Claire – but there's no sound insulation in these cabins and why would anyone come all the way up here if not for the quiet, couldn't they have gone to Newcastle or wherever it is people go for clubbing and gigs these days if they want that kind of thing? And with the little girl, too, Claire saw her still running around dressed like a little – well, inappropriately dressed – long after midnight. She hopes there's someone with her in the evenings, that she's not being left to fend for herself while her mum's behind the bar. Safe enough here, no doubt, not as if there's much worry about strangers and plenty of folk she could ask for help. Claire heard her playing with those other kids down on the beach earlier today though the boy was pretending to have a gun and it didn't sound very nice, if it hadn't been raining so hard she might have strolled down there just to cast an eye over whatever was going on. You never know what will cross kids' minds to try, those S2s at Jon's last school who spent the lunchtime after their Physics lesson on electricity seeing if they could hack the safety features on a socket. She should pop over maybe, just to say they are neighbours after all and if the little girl ever needs anything while her mum's at work, though maybe they'd take that the wrong way, interfering and passing judgement. Which she is, really. Not that kids don't die for lack of interference and passing judgement, all those cases where decent folk minded their own business while the neighbours beat and starved their children behind the net curtains. Quite ordinary people, sometimes. It takes a village to raise a child, isn't that what they say? Someone has to be the village, to say what's normal.

Mummy, Izzie's saying, Mummy, that boy was almost falling over, he nearly dropped his boat, look. Oh well, Claire says, he's back home now, with his mum. What will it be like, having the children leave and return, use their keys in the door and come in from the street bearing their own lives like ordinary people? Well, but they'll be different children by then, won't they, different people. Her too, probably, and Jon, coming up fifty. Fifty! Assuming we're all still here by then, assuming no demented President has pressed his big red button and there is still air to breathe and water to drink. It was inexcusable, really, to have children, the way things are, the way they're going to be. Iz, she says, give Mummy a hug, and Izzie eyes her, sizing up the damage she's being asked to repair, and Claire drops to her knees so the hug is where she needs it, on her chest, against her heart. She squeezes until Izzie's ribcage flexes. There, says Izzie, all better, and she pats Claire's shoulder and returns to the window, as if there's something out there for her.

Claire goes back to the sink. The half-hearted job Izzie would make of the glass isn't worth the argument. The cabin was supposed to have been cleaned before they arrived and goodness knows they've paid enough for it, it's really not on, cleaners who don't do behind the taps, you don't expect to have to spend your holiday cleaning. She's going to have a proper go at the cupboard doors too, there've been sticky fingers there, not to mention the handle of the grill, and if there's time the light switches as well, lots of people don't clean them at all though everyone's touching them all the time. She'll be more relaxed, once she knows it's all clean, or at least that the dirt is theirs.

The wailing hiccups and stops. Jon's coming through, Patrick in his arms reaching out to Claire with tears still on his red face. Sorry, says Jon, nothing's working, he just doesn't seem sleepy. Mummy, says Patrick, Mummy, and Claire rinses her hands and takes him. He clenches his legs on her hip and touches her face with a sad sticky finger; Jon's right, if he were really tired he'd be lying on her shoulder and probably kneading her boob. It was just feeling mean, Jon says, keeping him in the cot when he didn't want to be there. Lots of parenting, Claire thinks, feels mean, that's why adults have to do it, prioritising long-term outcomes over the emotions of the moment. Prioritising long-term outcomes, there's a phrase she hasn't used in nearly five years. Does that woman still exist, the one who wore dry-clean-only clothes and put together presentations? The software will have changed since then, not to mention the clothes. Claire strokes Patrick's hair. Come on then, she says, are you not a sleepy bunny? Shall we find the farm?

She brought a whole plastic storage box of toys from home, trying to choose those of interest to both children, which is an efficient use of space and/or a recipe for fights. If you really pay attention, you can build a farm on which Izzie can take the cows in for milking or – the new favourite – borrow the wolf from the zoo to run amok while Pat presses the buttons that make the brown cows moo in spectral tones. She'd thought they might see real Highland cows this week, maybe standing in the water the way they do in all those postcards and jigsaw puzzles, but if there are any they have sensibly been inside all week. Izzie, she says, shall we build a farm? She carries Pat over to the toybox and kneels down, tries not to let herself think that all they've achieved by spending so much money to be away from home for two weeks is to deprive themselves of the usual resources for passing the time: resources such as the swimming pool, which is hellish while you're doing it but worth it afterwards when the kids are exhausted and most of the day has gone by the time you've reached it on the bus with the buggy and got both of them and yourself changed and put things in lockers and let Izzie have the key pinned on her costume and taken her to pee and inflated all the armbands and helped both of them into the water and played at mummy and baby seals or water pixies or whatever and praised Izzie's doggy-paddle and applauded when Pat propels himself half a metre and remembered how you used to swim miles, up and down, tumble turns as you'd learnt at school, twice a week before work, just silent swimming with other silent swimmers, and lifted them both out of the water which is tricky, like that puzzle with the chicken and the fox in the boat, and gone back to the changing room and through the shower and put them into dry clothes and then sorted yourself, double quick, don't really bother drying because it's while you're vulnerable without your knickers or your glasses that one of them's going to go drown itself, and then persuaded or wrestled Pat back into the pushchair and swept the area for toys and stray hairbands and flaccid armbands and walked back towards the bus, both children now whiney, needing biscuits you packed earlier and patience and tact while you pray that there isn't already a buggy on the bus, kept them occupied while you waited, nursery rhymes and good cheer, and more on the bus, singing very quietly the wheels on the bus go round and round, lurching through the same old streets, round and round, round and round. And here, she thinks, setting out the plastic fences, we must make our own fun. She must make their own fun.

Claire, says Jon, Claire, what if I take them out for a bit, he might sleep in the pushchair and if he doesn't at least it's some fresh air and a change of scene, and Izzie's got her boots and puddle suit. She looks up at him. It's pouring, she says. He shrugs. We've got coats. They can jump in the bath when we get back. It couldn't be for long, anyway, but you'd like an hour to yourself, wouldn't you? Have your own bath. Worse come to the worst I can take them to the pub for juice, it's not the end of the world. No, she says, no, I know, but it's meant to be a holiday for you too. Jon smiles at Izzie, who beams back. It is a holiday for me, he says, I don't see much of them, during term. What do you say, Iz, shall we go jump in puddles? You can even paddle a bit, in your wellies. Yay, says Izzie, raising her arms, yay paddling. Pat, Claire knows, won't like it, doesn't have wellies, can't balance on the stony beach, he'll want out of the pushchair and then Jon will need two hands for him and two more to be able to catch Izzie or rescue her if she falls, but it's not as if she hasn't dealt with these things often enough this last year and Jon is, after all, a teacher, albeit teenagers not toddlers, has more training than she does in doing stuff with kids. I could get this place properly clean, she thinks, I could, indeed, have a bath, maybe we could have a nice dinner after the kids are in bed, or if not exactly nice at least different from theirs, didn't I see a candle in that cupboard for all there are the signs about open flames and fire risk? A bath, she thinks, and later a candlelit dinner, and no marking for Jon to do, almost like a real holiday. We could talk, about something or other, not the children, and then maybe later— You sure, she says, and Jon says, yes, of course I'm sure, it's an hour, babe, have a nap or a bath or paint your toenails, whatever you want. Go to the pub for the wifi, if you like. Have a drink. He grins. Have a cocktail with a sparkler in it.

She used to like cocktails, once, that woman in the dry-clean-only jackets and the high heels. She used to redo her make-up in the office loos and go straight on to a bar. Sometimes, on Fridays, several bars.

Come on, Izzie, Jon says, see if you can put on your puddle suit and wellies before I get Pat into the pushchair.

There's a flurry of boots and waterproofs, a fresh nappy for Pat, a pot of breadsticks in case he needs distraction in the pushchair, Jon's implausibly large waterproof trousers, a tussle with Izzie who wants to take her purple umbrella and is adamant that she doesn't need to pee until she changes her mind after the puddle suit is zipped up, and then they are gone.

She closes the door.

It's quiet.

It's still quiet.

There's wind, of course, and the rain on the roof, but she can hear her own breathing. She coughs, to make a sound. Right then, she thinks, Jon didn't give her this hour to listen to her own lungs. She has sixty minutes, more or less, to do anything at all, to please herself. She remembers those oceans of time, in London before the children, the weekends and evenings she didn't even notice, wasted messing around on the internet, watching shows that weren't quite boring enough to turn off, looking at stuff she wasn't going to buy and places she wasn't going to visit. Not that she didn't also cook for friends and go out dancing and to films and concerts. Which is not the point, because there's no internet here as well as no friends, and the last thing she wants is to go to the pub, full of damp and depressed young foreign hikers and certainly without cocktail sparklers or probably even cocktail glasses, not that she wants to drink at this hour.

She could dance, she supposes, could be the kind of woman who dances when nobody's watching, but with the French windows you can't ever really be sure that nobody's watching, she sometimes thinks everyone on the park is spending their entire holidays watching each other, and anyway if she wants to dance she can do it with Izzie, sometimes when she doesn't want to dance she still does it with Izzie, for whom she should find a proper class in September. Ballet, she thinks, remembering her own pink silk shoes and a net skirt she pretended was a tutu, a pink 'ballet wrap' knitted by her grandmother who died while Claire was pregnant with Izzie. Gran wanted to hold out to see the first great-grandchild and failed by six weeks, Claire waddling at the funeral, trying not to let her grief seep through her bloodstream and into the baby's unformed brain. She's sure she read somewhere recently that they think sadness crosses the placenta, more or less, that a woman who is frightened or upset or depressed in pregnancy steeps her developing child in sorrow, setting up a lifetime of misery. Not that Izzie seems given to misery: irritation, perhaps. Impatience. And such an unfair thing to say, it's not as if women go round being frightened and upset and depressed on purpose, what are you supposed to do if disarray and death come calling, what if things are, in fact, frightening? Anyway, Claire says out loud, come on, you've already spent about three minutes just standing about. If she's just going to stand here she might as well get on with the cleaning, but that's not what Jon meant, he'll be disappointed, feel his gift rejected, if he gets back and finds that's all she's done. Have a bath, he said, seeming to forget that she doesn't actually like baths all that much. Women's magazines always say that, a long scented bath, as if everything from baby weight to infidelity will dissolve in enough hot water, as if you can spend enough on bath salts to cover the smell of self-loathing and repressed rage. Baths, in Claire's opinion, are pretty boring, too hot until they're too cold and there's not much you can do in there, they're not exactly comfortable for reading, your neck always at the wrong angle and your magazine going sticky in the steam. She'll have a look for the candle, anyway, while she decides. She'd like that candlelit dinner.

But first she goes over to the window, leans against it to see as far as possible towards the shore. They've left the pushchair tilted disturbingly under the trees and there's Jon with Pat on his hip – say what you like for feminism, men aren't built to carry babies – and Izzie picking something up and showing it to him. Her breath is misting the glass and she swipes it with her sleeve. Stones, must be. Jon swaps Pat to his left arm and makes the tennis motion of someone skipping a stone across the water, and she can see from his shrug and the way he turns to Izzie that it didn't fly; sank, in fact, like a stone, and Izzie squats down with a seriousness she will lose any day now, the seriousness accorded to the ground under our feet only by toddlers and botanists, and passes him another. That's all right then, Claire thinks. Let's find that candle, although it's true that finding a candle is something she could do with all of them around, the kind of thing that might sometimes pass as a game for Izzie. Hunt the Candle. So it's a waste of the hour Jon's giving her, to look for a lost object, or possibly, in this case, an object that was never there in the first place, the memory of which may in fact come from some other holiday cottage because this is the only kind of holiday they've had since Izzie was born, she didn't need friends to tell her that babies and hotels weren't going to lead to relaxation and joy and hot sex, good heavens why is she thinking about sex again, she must tell Jon, it's coming back, that's at least twice already today which probably means her reproductive cycle is restarting at last and she doesn't have any tampons, though as far as she can remember the days of wanting sex come around ten days before the bleeding, how it can take an egg ten days to travel about five centimetres she has never understood, but she knows from the babies that there's somehow no gravity in there, or at least not until you stand up and find that your period started or your waters broke while you were sitting down. Buy tampons, she thinks, no great rush but next time we're at the shops, must remember to ask Jon to remind me. At least they do have plenty of nappies if she needs to improvise a pad, and there must be scissors in the house. Look for scissors, she thinks, but she doesn't need them now and that's not what this hour is for, crafting your own sanitary towels. What else did Jon say, paint your toenails? She does, occasionally, in summer, she and Izzie together choosing which of their twenty toes should have which colour but she is unlikely to be wearing sandals any day soon, not least because she didn't bring them here, and anyway it's another thing that Izzie would enjoy too, and anyway she didn't bring any nail polish either – well, why would you, really – so she's just wasted about another two minutes of her hour.

Still, she thinks, still, if they are going to have sex later, there's certainly a little titivating could be done. She puts her hand up her jumper – cold hand – to check her armpit, which she can't have shaved for a few days, and then she remembers that hair on her areola, the big black one that comes back. She did deal with it religiously while breastfeeding, who would want that in his mouth with his milk, but lately – she goes into the bathroom where there's a mirror and lifts the jumper and takes out her left boob, which goes all perky in the cold. Not so bad, she thinks, considering, considering it wasn't that exciting to start with. She strokes her nipple and the breast's round underside, feels the other one wake up too. Yes, she thinks, yes, they are hers again. She must tell Jon. But the hair is there, and alarmingly long. She tries to use her fingernails as tweezers although it almost never works, just bends the nails which are softer than they probably should be anyway, she needs more protein or calcium or B vitamins or whatever it is, doesn't like supplements because they're just an excuse for a poor diet which would be a reasonable position if she then took to eating kale or almonds or oily fish – horrible oily fish with bones and slime and a mess that has to go straight to the outside bin and a smell that lives under the stairs for days – but is mildly self-destructive when paired with a diet persistently based on tea and toast and the children's leftovers. Buy a multivitamin supplement, she thinks, along with the tampons, either that or eat some kale, as if she doesn't know perfectly well that the choice licenses inaction: it's not that she's deciding not to address the problem, just that at any given moment she is inclining towards one solution and therefore not obliged to act on the other. And meanwhile she really does need the tweezers, which she knows are in the First Aid kit because you need them for removing ticks and it is a foolish person who goes to the Scottish hills without a means of removing ticks. But the First Aid kit, she's pretty sure, is in the car, and she doesn't want Jon and Izzie to see her rummaging in the car, they'll come and help and she'll have to explain that she does not in fact require First Aid but only — no, she thinks, no, even she will have a moment to herself in the bathroom later, before any sex is at all possible, and she'll deal with the hair then. Unless she can get it out with her fingernails. Or her teeth, can she reach the top of her areola with her teeth? She did once try to suck her own milk, when her breasts were engorged after Izzie was born and she was weeping with the pain and the only effect of the cabbage leaves in the bra recommended by the midwife was the discovery of three small caterpillars in a place where a person does not expect to find caterpillars: well, said Jon, of course I bought organic cabbage, you don't want pesticides on your nipples for breastfeeding, do you? Very nearly, she can. She can stick her tongue out and touch the hair, which is as wiry and prickly as she thought.

Ow, her neck.

Right, Jon did not give her this hour for licking her own nipple hairs. She rubs her neck. She's a bit hungry, she thinks, she could have some chocolate, while Izzie's not here to want some and spoil her dinner and learn to associate sugar with treats. Or maybe she's just thirsty, she read somewhere that people often eat when really all they need is a drink of water, though she can drink as much water as she likes when the children are around, she's not wasting this hour drinking water. Oh, tea, she thinks, a lovely cup of tea drunk while still hot enough to scald a baby, that's what she should do. And a biscuit with it, one of those posh chocolate ones bought as a holiday treat along with the good olives and the croissants, although she shouldn't eat those on her own, they're for sharing, even Pat could probably have half of one to smear across his face. Tea, anyway, and she fills the kettle and turns it on and while she's waiting has another go at those taps and then wanders back to the window. They're still there, on the beach, Pat standing now grasping both of Jon's hands so that Jon has to stoop down in a way that hurts her back when she does it and must be agonising for him, a good six inches taller, and Izzie paddling in water closer to the top of her wellies than Claire would encourage, it would only take one bigger-than-most wave, not that it matters really, much, wet feet, Jon's right, the kids can have an afternoon bath if they get too cold, maybe hot chocolate, not, probably, that there is any hot chocolate, not unless someone else left some in that cupboard and it is the sort of thing people do leave in the cupboards of holiday cottages, but no, there isn't any and that handle really is sticky, how has she not noticed that before? She cleans the handle, and then while she's about it, while she has the spray and the cloth in her hand, the other handles, and the oven door, and the kettle boiled a while ago and she's not supposed to be cleaning.

Claire makes two cups of tea, in the biggest mugs she can find which are still annoyingly small and also tartan, not really what she'd call a proper cup of tea. She leaves them on the counter while she puts on her flowery water-proof mac-in-a-bag and the clashing flowery wellies that Izzie chose for her last birthday and then she goes out, sets the tea on the step where rain falls in it while she closes the front door, and carries the cups carefully over the gravel and grass and rocks down towards the shore. There's no one else out and you can see why, only with small children is it more fun to be out in this weather than inside with a book and a cup of tea, but if all the neigh-bours are indoors there are watchers at every window. There's that other English family, they're saying, did I tell you now he's a teacher in Edinburgh? Aye, it's full of Eng-lish these days, can't stand their own country any more. You'd tell a mile off, wouldn't you, him in that green jacket and all. Her feet slide around in her purple tulip wellies, need an extra pair of socks really, and she can feel the stones through the soles and the rain on her face, coming through her hair already. Three more days to go, she thinks, and they won't come back here. The loch, maybe. Well, probably, it's hard to avoid if you're driving north of Glasgow and they've all Scotland to explore these coming years, but not here. They've seen it now, no need to come again, and bubbles of relief rise in her head. Home soon, back to the flat with its wooden floors and the lovely old plasterwork even if it does need repainting, and the high ceilings. She's got used to living with all that airspace now, when they first moved in she felt exposed, dizzy, as if something might swoop down on her while she played on the floor with Izzie or lay in her own bed but now she's hemmed in when there's no headroom. The stones hurt her feet through the rubber soles. Rain mists her glasses. No, they won't come back here.

Patrick sees her first, and his excitement makes Jon turn and Izzie wave so hard she almost loses her balance in the water. Mummy, she says, Mummy, look, and Jon, Patrick in one arm and takes the tea in the other hand, gives her a kiss on the cheek. Pat lurches, casts himself onto the air between his parents, spills his father's tea. They won't always love her this much, she thinks, holding her son, no one else, not even her children's future selves, will ever be so pleased to see her coming as they are today.

the weight of water

The light is as it was this morning. These midsummer days move too slowly to see, especially with the curtains of rain and cloud closed upon the woods and shore. Huddled in a hazel bush, a short-eared owl waits, unseen. If it does not hunt soon it will die but if it flies now the weight of water will drag it to the ground where dusk will bring harm: foxes, humans and still nothing to eat. A vole now, even a pipit or sparrow, would buy the owl more hours of life, more time for the rain to stop.

once there stood

SHE CAN'T FIND it.

There's always one in her drawing bag, kicking around with the paper pad and the pencil case, and usually another in the box, but today there isn't. She must have had one in the café, mustn't she, she can't have made that whole sketch without. Probably. Try to use it less, Annie says in the weekly group, just draw what you see the way you see it, don't be always correcting and second-guessing yourself. It's funny how you can't avoid taking art lessons personally.

You'd think that maybe people, the over-fifty-fives, would paint with their unconsciousnesses, their repressed selves or what have you. You'd think, or maybe hope, that the quiet wives in pastel jumpers and beige make-up would splash scarlet and crimson and slash black lines, that the ones in long skirts and flat shoes would betray a passion for order in neat little pencil sketches, and perhaps that the two men – chinos under eight-month bellies

– would show a turn for raging dancers and stormy skies. People do, sometimes, betray the wildness they carry in their heads. The older she is, the more she thinks everyone's at it, because it turns out that being a little old lady doesn't stop you wanting to bash the panels of cars parked on the pavement with your umbrella and snatch and stamp on the phones of people having loud conversations on the bus. Quite recently at the supermarket Mary was in the queue behind a lass who was expecting, she'd asked when the bairn was due, just touched the bump, so round and taut, and the lass told her where to go in terms she's not going to repeat and then started crying, right there by the cereal bars, and though she was shocked and upset Mary also felt a wee surge of admiration. It's cheering, somehow, when it's the unlikely people quietly amok, Sheila Hepton up the road, mother of three boys and kept the house so neat you didn't want to sit down for fear of squashing a cushion, never seen without lipstick and foundation in thirty years of neighbourliness, turned out she'd been at it with Alan's boss for years, up to all sorts Mary hadn't even heard of until Jeannie next door told her. There's no reason, really, why high standards in make-up and housework should indicate high standards of morality, after all don't we all go deeper than mascara and folded towels, but still. Not that Mary approves, not that she really considers that sort of thing admirable, better to splash paint or take up cycling or even sell up and buy a ruined farmhouse out in the hills and spend ten years rewiring and plastering and plumbing like the McVeys than ruin your marriage for a man no more handsome or interesting than your husband, and honestly in Mary's view after a few years no one's going to be more handsome or interesting than your husband; setting aside the violent and deranged, getting married is like voting in that whatever you choose the outcome will be at best mildly unsatisfactory four years down the line. Anyway, turns out most people don't express their secret selves on paper but draw exactly what you'd expect from looking at them, you could see someone on a bus and make a perfectly accurate assumption about her artistic tendencies, which is why she needs the thing. The whatsit. She likes to get things right. She doesn't want to improvise around mistakes, she wants it done properly in the first place. And it was here, it was definitely here, and now it's not, and she never loses things, never ever, and it can't have just vanished, it's not as if there are children or even a cat to move things around.

She knows it's not in her handbag, there's no reason it would be and she's already looked twice, but she's now, she thinks, into the ritual phase of looking for something. Leaning on the back of her chair as she passes, she carries the handbag over to the table. Her younger self would have upended it, let everything cascade over the tablecloth. Maybe her younger self would have painted differently too, but she'll never know what she might have done if she hadn't been a doctor's wife and the mother of Melissa and Marcus. She pulls out a chair and sits down, and David, reading a book on the future of the country in his armchair, looks up and asks what she's doing. You mind your own business, she wants to say, but she says, oh, just going through my bag, it's getting a bit heavy. Looking for the thing. Looking for the word for the thing. He'd only worry, or take her off to the doctor, and they can't do anything, can they, about – well, about this kind of thing. If that's what it is.

He grunts and looks out of the window. She thinks he's not really all that interested in that book, which looks to be another five-hundred-page lump by another – what's the word – preposterous, propensity, no, the other one, wealthy, well off, ha, *prosperous*, that's it, another prosperous *and* preposterous Englishman about how the world is ending because no one's doing what the writer thinks they ought to do, learning obsolete words for insects or scrubbing floors on their hands and knees with wooden brushes or exposing babies to germs, usually something the writer imagines that women or the lower orders did before he was born. She doesn't know why David goes on buying them. Keeps the old brain ticking over, he says, as if hers isn't, as if all that walking about in the rain and reading tedious books will stop him getting old and dying like everyone else. Anyway, she can't sit about here all day. Why is her handbag on the table, she doesn't like bags on tables, not once they've been on the floors of cafés and ferries and even public loos, you wouldn't put your shoes on the dinner table, would you? She stands up slowly and leans on the table while the cabin around her tilts, wobbles. It's not dramatic, the way the earth moves lately. There are no earthquakes or bombs, just an instability, as if all the surfaces are delicately balanced and easily tipped. The children had toys like that, Weebles, they were called, egg-shaped people about three inches tall and you could force them all the way down to the ground and they'd spring up lurching from side to side and eventually sway themselves upright. Like one of those things that hangs from a big clock, the ticker.

She takes the handbag over to her armchair and bends her knees to put it on the floor, which is one of the places she might think to look next time she wants it. It's not easy, standing up again, even holding on to the chair back. Things aren't always exactly where she thinks they are these days, as if everything is out of the corner of her eye, as if her hands and feet are guessing a bit. Outside, she sees, down by the water, there's that nice family staying in number five, the baby boy and the little girl with about the same gap as Marcus and Melissa. She and David hadn't bought the cabin then, not until David's dad died when Marcus was four – well, the cabins weren't even built, the holiday park was just woodland like everywhere up here though the pub is old, her dad remembered walking up to the pub while the road was still a track and the deliveries came by boat. Did they go on holiday, when the children were so young? She doesn't think so, just family visits, mostly her parents because they could see David's every Sunday anyway, and David not always with them. He used to work so hard. She took the children on the train, she remembers it now, and prams were so big in those days, handy for the shopping and good in the weather but you couldn't be always popping them into cars and lifting them on and off buses and trains the way people do now, she just used to carry Marcus in her arms and Melissa trotting alongside and were there still porters, then, for the luggage? David, she says, were there still porters, do you remember, on trains when the children were little, or did people help you when you needed it? What, he says, lowering the book. Porters, she says, when did there stop being porters on the trains? I have no idea, he says.

The young man down there, the father, is holding two mugs and he's smiling and talking to his wife and the baby has wrapped himself around the girl and lain his head on her shoulder. She remembers that weight, the lolling hardness and the smell of baby hair. There won't be grandchildren, she thinks, which is silly, the ages people have babies now there's still time, even for Melissa, though Melissa's babies will presumably be in – in that place. One of Queen Victoria's daughters, and not New Zealand but the other one. And Marcus is, what, coming up forty-five which would be fine if he were married, or even living with someone, but if you allow at least a couple of years for all that and assume that she's not much younger than him, time's running out. They said Mary was an 'elderly primigravida' back in the day, waiting for David to qualify and get set up in practice, but by today's standards – Melissa does have a boyfriend, they've seen him on the computer, a man with a beard and one of those New World names that's really a surname, or quite often a town. Warwick, that's it. Imagine looking at your baby and thinking, let's call him Warwick. Do they even know how to pronounce it? War-wick. War, candle-wicks, candlesticks, they've some around here somewhere, candlesticks, in case of power cuts, must be candles too, surely, you wouldn't have just the candlesticks. Pewter, with handles like teacups. She'd like to know what the children on the shore are called, hopes they have real names of the sort that served everyone just fine for centuries, saints and the Old Testament, Romans and Greeks, forebears. Melissa, she'd probably just be called Honey these days. They do these things better in France, with that list of names acceptable to the state, stops people who don't know any better being ridiculous, though trust the bloody French, wasn't there some trouble over Mohammed? Still, there won't be any French babies called Chardonnay. Miel, wouldn't it be, like a vacuum cleaner? Something like that. She remembers Melissa with two plaits and a missing front tooth, *je m'appelle Melissa, j'ai huit ans, j'habite à Bearsden avec mon père, ma mère et mon frère.* There, some things you don't forget. Test me again, Mummy, I got ten out of ten last time. The things we learn to say first: here I am. I announce myself. My name is Mary, I am – well, it doesn't matter, does it? Getting on. Not dead yet. *Je suis, tu es, il est. Nous sommes, vous êtes, ils sont.* See? She even remembers the accents. *Circonflexe.* And she can still do poetry, *Deep asleep, deep asleep, Deep asleep it lies, The still lake of Summerwater Under the still skies.* Herself in little white socks and the dress her mother made, real Liberty lawn with the red berries on it, stepping forward on the stage and seeing her parents in the middle of the front row, smiling, Dad mouthing along with her, Mum in that hat. No, *Semmerwater,* not *summerwater,* took her ages to remember to say it right, Dad listening to her every night when he came back from work, and here she is getting it wrong again sixty years later. Or sixty-five. *Once there stood by Semmerwater, A mickle town and tall; King's tower and Queen's bower, And wakeman on the wall.* Then what? *Came a beggar, halt and sore, 'I faint for lack of bread.' King's tower and Queen's bower, Cast him forth unfed.* There, all the words, she can still do it. And then the shepherd feeds the beggar. *They gave him of their oatcake, they gave him of their ale.* And then? The rhythm goes odd, she remembers that, the lines stretch out. Something about *glimmer of scale* and *gleam of fin, weed and reed in the gloom. And a lost city in Summerwater* – Semmerwater – *deep asleep till Doom.* An odd choice, really, for a young child, though people worried less about that kind of thing in those days. And she still knows the songs, doesn't she, most of the hymnary, she'd be willing to bet, second and third verses too. *They stand, those halls of Zion, Conjubilant with song.* Has anyone ever said *conjubilant*? One of those hymn words. And Christmas carols, the music teacher didn't like them to be holding papers so they learnt everything, all the verses, even if you weren't in the choir you had to do it. *And our eyes at last shall see him, Through his own redeeming love. For that child, so dear and gentle, Is our Lord in Heaven above.* The floor tilts and she rests a hand on the curtain as she sings quietly to herself, *And he leads his children on, To the place where he is gone.* Flickering candles, cold stone underfoot, the scent of pine on the air.

The mother has perched herself on a rock now, with the baby on her knee and what's probably the mug balanced at her side, not really a good idea when the mugs belong to the lodge and they'll surely have to pay for breakages. The father is showing the little girl how to skim stones although he's not very good at it himself. We were like that, Mary thinks, we were just like that, although she's not sure she can remember a single occasion when David had time to play outside with the baby and the toddler. He must have done. Maybe it happened so often it wasn't memorable. And later, certainly, once he was settled in General Practice, there were sometimes days off, he used to take himself out hill-walking, all weathers. She did see his point, he was working all week, on call half the weekends and why shouldn't he have a day to himself, it wasn't every week, but once the children were at school she could have gone with him if he'd been willing to come back mid-afternoon. She'd have liked it, a few hours up the Campsies between washing up the breakfast and going back to the school gates. The father is taking the child's hand, showing her how to reach back and then skite the stone over the waves.

Why did she come over here, anyway? What time is it? The light never changes, these dull summer days, hour after hour of grey pallor seeping through the trees, the sky at breakfast no different from bedtime. Still raining. Coming up five. If she makes something complicated for tea, it could be time to start cooking, or at least arranging things ready to cook. She made a plan when they went to the shops, wrote out a list of meals and ingredients. There was fish, wasn't there, in the freezer? And potatoes, new potatoes in the summer, and you're allowed to eat butter again now after all those years when it would kill you just to look at the wrapper. There's mint in a pot on the veranda, and she remembers buying courgettes. She could scrub the potatoes now, and pick the mint, and maybe say hello to that nice family if they happen to come back while she's out there, find out the names and all.

Mary unlocks the French window, but the key doesn't work. David looks at her over the top of his book. It's already open, he says, what are you going out there for?

She doesn't know. She doesn't know why she's opening the door, and the weather the way it is. Where is she going? Everything turns.

Deep breath.

To pick leaves, she says, for the potatoes. She tries to pull the door and it doesn't work, but when she turns the other way and pushes, it slides and the afternoon comes in, damp and chill.

David's put his book in his lap. Leaves, he says.

She makes a laugh. Oh, you know, she says, for the potatoes, you've always liked them like that. Butter and a bit of what's-it.

Mint, he says. Butter and mint. We haven't had herbs out there for years, Mary. Don't you remember, even when we had the pots right up by the window the rabbits got them all?

Now that he mentions it, she does, yes. She made unseasonal garlands of holly and hawthorn which had no apparent effect at all. Squirrels, more likely, she says, I doubt the rabbits could have climbed up on the table. Oh well then, no mint.

No, he says, no mint today.

He is still looking at her.

She does not look back.

where the bodies lie

In the shelter of the big pine tree there's an anthill, and within the anthill is a city. Within the city are many chambers: nurseries, granaries, the throne room and a crypt where the bodies lie, and within the chambers are worker ants, two hundred thousand of them, and the winged queen.

The city is south-facing for warmth, its roof angled like a solar panel to intercept the sun's rays at right angles. The temperature is falling and a team is moving the new brood into a warmer room. Their city is well built and they're safe enough from the weather, the settlement thatched like the roof of a Japanese palace to guide the rain from one panel to the next, to direct it downhill and away through the soil to the loch.

They close the entrances and wait.

what it's like being

DON'T USE THAT, says Mum, you'll scratch the tray, it's non-stick, that. Becky drops the wire scrubber into the washing-up bowl, which is full of brown water with squashed peas and bits of potato bobbling against her hands. Well how do you want me to clean it, then, she says. Elbow grease, says Mum, which is what she always says, and mind out, I want to get the kettle on.

Becky rubs at the tray, whose non-stick has been coming unstuck for years, with the brush. There are bits of yesterday's onion tangled in the bristles and she's not going to pick them out. I want to be dead, she hears in her head, I want to be dead. She's already washed the 'sharp knife' which isn't sharp at all, skids off tomatoes and inflicts blunt-force trauma on cheese, and anyway it's as hard to kill yourself with a knife as it is, apparently, easy to kill someone else. They had a prevention session at school, led by this seriously hot guy with dreadlocks who'd been in prison and didn't want any of them to have his life and Preti and that lot sat at the back and giggled.

I want to be dead.

In America, she knows, you can get the police to shoot you just by acting a bit weird with your hands in your pockets, which is a bummer if you're a weirdo with cold hands but must save suicidal people a lot of time and trouble. There's no way she's going to get the burnt-on fish off this tray with the brush, it's completely pointless, what Mum's making her do. Do get on with it, says Mum, it'll take you all night at this rate, doesn't have to be such a performance, you know. The kettle boils and Mum reaches round Becky – too close, unwashed hair and that awful hippy deodorant – for her box of herbal teabags. She chooses one each night, as if they weren't all the same anyway, as if dead leaves and hot water constitute some kind of celebration. Mum opens the box and stands there pushing her nose into it. It's her holiday treat, the selection box, at home she just buys supermarket chamomile, smelling of wet hay and loose because teabags are bad for the environment, which means that Mum's special treat is to destroy the planet Becky's going to inherit. Mmm, she says, now I'm saving the last of the cinnamon ones, I suppose I should have the lemon and ginger, I'm going to have to drink it sometime, but maybe mint and fennel tonight. Becky could wreck Mum's whole system of self-punishments and rewards by making herself a cup of apple and elderflower tea one morning. Buy a bottle of wine, she thinks, or vodka. Go down the pub and get off your face on Baileys. Eat a whole tub of fucking ice-cream but stop wetting yourself over the teabags, Jesus Christ. Mind out, she says, I thought you wanted me to finish the washing up. No need to take that tone, says Mum, opening the little paper envelope as if there might be a golden ticket inside it, almost kissing her disgusting teabag. What tone, mutters Becky, and when Mum doesn't respond, how do you know what tone I need.

I want to be dead.

She's not going to get the burnt fish off the tray without taking the non-stick surface with it and anyway what does it matter what's on a baking tray once it reaches 200C, surely that's enough to sterilise whatever's survived washing up. She goes on swishing the brush around until Mum's settled herself in her armchair – if she gets to be that old, Becky will kill herself the day she first groans on sitting down – and then tips out the mucky water, runs the tray under the tap, watching a rainbow film of oil glisten and flow, and balances it behind the pile of more-or-less clean dishes on the draining board. She's going to go see the soldier again, she thinks, because even hanging out with a weirdo in a wet tent is better than this. Being dead would be better than this. And he's not that weird, actually, Gavin, he grew up in Lennoxtown, went to the Academy, normal enough, it's just that then he joined the Army and ended up fighting in Iraq, though he won't tell her what the fighting was about. Oil, he says. Money. Politicians in London telling lies. You don't want to know. He stops looking at her when she asks about Iraq but she tried it anyway, what was it like then, out there? Did you kill anyone, she wanted to ask, because imagine crouching in a tent with a man who has killed someone and why else do soldiers go places, but she didn't quite have the nerve. I don't talk about that, he said, you need to get off home now lassie. Next time she took him a pack of biscuits from the cupboard and chatted about the weather and how weird it is on the park, the way everyone's watching each other and there's nothing to do and somehow this is meant to be more fun than being at home. He was definitely happier talking about her life than his, even made eye-contact once or twice. Don't leave it like that, says Mum, everything'll fall off, have a bit of sense. Some of it wants drying and putting away, you can't always wander off and leave everything. I'm not trying to wander off, says Becky, I was just putting the tray down. Well, now you can pick it up, says Dad, and dry it and put it away the way Mum's telling you. She wants to scream. She wants to throw the fucking tray at the wall. I washed up, she says, Alex can dry and put away. Oh for goodness' sake, says Mum, Rob, you deal with her, and Dad stands up. Rebecca, can you just for once do as you're told, can we just for once have one peaceful hour before bedtime without you whining and bickering. Your mother cooked for you, you're too old for this, you're acting like a spoilt child, you can't expect to be waited on hand and foot, now take that cloth and dry those dishes and put them away or there'll be trouble, do you understand? No, she thinks, actually I don't, I don't understand any of it, all this fuss about teabags and washing up, it's not normal, normal parents would just be grateful I'm not taking drugs or sleeping around. Normal parents would be grateful she's actually here with them in the stupid cabin in the middle of fucking nowhere, none of her friends have to do this stuff. Trouble like what, she says, and Dad looks at Mum and sighs and sits down again. Trouble like you won't like, he says, trouble like not having any money and not being allowed to go out and if you really push it, trouble like not having a phone. Becks, can you just finish the job.

There isn't anywhere to go out, she says, who even wants to go out, and in case you haven't noticed phones are basically useless here, I'm not even taking photos because who wants to remember this, I can't exactly post, can I, more rain on more trees, rain again, trees again, more rain, more trees, hashtag summer holiday, hashtag family fun.

Oh shush, says Dad, enough. I'm a man of many powers but even for you I can't control the weather. Promise you, princess, when I can make the sun shine, I will. Now dry the dishes, Becks, please.

Becky picks up the damp tea towel with a map of the loch on it and dries the tray. She's definitely going to go see Gavin, assuming he's there but where else would he be, a day like today, though he does go out in the rain. You'd have to, wouldn't you, can't lie in a tent all day. He picks berries, he's got these grubby big glass jars with the labels peeling off them, probably from the pub, Branston pickle and mayonnaise, full of bilberries and also orange rowans which don't even look edible, but he must get some money from somewhere because there are also sweetie wrappers and tins of stew, the really cheap own-brand stuff from the supermarket at the foot of the loch. If Mum and Dad weren't always here she could make him some sandwiches.

Some black stuff she hadn't noticed comes off onto the towel, but it needed a wash anyway. Dad did take her phone for a week when they spied on her and found out she'd been posting stuff during lessons, which was school's fault the classes were so boring and also school's fault because if the teachers don't even notice half the class on their phones they're clearly not paying much attention either and they're the ones getting paid. So she took his phone from his jacket pocket and held it hostage for hers and he went through her room when she was out and found his phone but also some private things and she was so angry she banged her head on the wall in front of him and he yelled at her that she was crazy and hysterical and then they didn't talk for several days until she found her phone on her bed one afternoon when she came home from school, with a stupid mushy note from Dad.

Mum sniffs and then slurps her tea and sighs. She can't possibly be tired, they haven't done anything this whole week. Though Becky is tired, she thinks, she would like to get under her duvet and stay there for days, until the end of this alleged holiday, until the season in her head changes and she feels like getting up and maybe that will be never. She watched one of Dad's stupid wildlife documentaries with him once, she can't remember why, must have been really bored, and there was this Arctic vole thing that sleeps about nine months of the year and is basically nearly dead, its heart beating like four beats a minute, just enough to stop the blood congealing in its veins, only every few days it has to wake up enough to shiver for about half an hour so it doesn't completely die, and if she could do that, she thinks, if she could be just not-dead until she's grown up, then maybe she could keep going. Though then you'd wake up at eighteen with no Highers, and if the teachers are right you'd be better off dead anyway.

She pushes the tray into the oven so that it bangs against the back and while Mum is still jumping she slams the oven door. There, she says, OK, can I go now or would you maybe like me to scrub the floor first? Well, says Dad, if you're offering now, sure, go ahead, but Mum says, Rob, don't tease her, yes, Becks, go on, why don't you go join Alex at the pub, we can run to a couple of quid for a bottle of ginger. Take your phone, catch up with your friends. Join *Alex* at the *pub*, she thinks, you have to be fucking kidding, plus it's still pissing it down out there so she can't even just go hang around the beer garden for the wifi and also she doesn't really feel like going on her phone any more, it's not as if she has anything to tell anyone. Still raining. Still bored. Still sharing a room with my brother, eww. Becky hasn't actually seen Jamila for months; her parents finally managed to move to India, 'back to India', they say, better opportunities there for the children these days, but it's not back anywhere for Jamila and she doesn't want better opportunities, she just wants her friends. Even so, she's seeing the world, isn't she? It's better to be complaining about hot weather and nosy aunties than rain and your mum's stupid hippy tea. Tanya's mum's paying her (not enough) to look after her little brothers, Megan's at home and actually having the best time of any of them because her parents are out at work all day and her sister left home last year so she can basically do what she likes, which is sleep all morning and upload videos of herself making her own face packs out of weird stuff she buys from the wholefood shop.

I still don't see why we can't get wifi here, Becky says, leaning against the counter so it digs into her hip and hurts, then we wouldn't have to be always going off to the pub, you know Alex is going to try to buy beer one of these days, you're basically driving us to drink, I bet you can get weed in that pub as well if you know who to ask and you're always telling us it's not like the stuff that was around when you were our age, what if he gets hallucinations and paranoia and goes bipolar, won't you wish you'd just paid for broadband? I'm not having the wifi conversation again, says Mum, you can come and sit here with us if you'll stop complaining for half an hour or you can go to your room or you can go to the pub. Those are your options. Oh no they're not, Becky thinks, you have no idea, and I hate you, I never asked to be born, you have no idea what it's like being a teenager now seeing as there wasn't even like Facebook when you were young, but she said pretty much exactly that last week and her parents shouted 'bingo' and laughed, and though they'd just proved her point Becky cried and then Mum was sorry and tried to hug her even though she was the one who'd made her cry in the first place. Fine, she says, and manages to get a good slam out of the bedroom door despite the thick carpet.

Becky drops face-down on her bed, though in a minute, she thinks, when she's finished, she is going to go find Gavin's tent. Hot night out or what? The mattress is harder than at home and it hurts her breasts, which are tender today. She presses her face into the pillow and wonders how people die of having pillows over their faces

– a pillow's not airtight, is it, she's breathing depressingly well through it so why can't everyone else? Like everything here, the pillow smells of plastic and mildew, the whole building, the whole shell of all their so-called holidays, tacky and temporary. Gimcrack, she thinks, and wonders how you pronounce it, jim-crack or the way it looks? Dad's said more than once, the whole thing would go up like paper in a fire, wouldn't pass regs these days, and it's not that she hasn't thought about it, thought that with one match, one of the ones in the box in the kitchen, she could end the whole thing. Light the curtains, which came from Gran's house when she moved and are so old they actually have holes in them which Mum says don't show but they do and they definitely pre-date fire-retardant, and it would all be over in a few minutes. Flames creeping and munching up the blue flowers, smoke smearing the damp-stained ceiling. The boiler's just along the wall and there's one gas cylinder attached outside and the spare in the outdoor cupboard against her and Alex's bedroom wall. Light that and your problems would soon be over.

Her face is getting hot. She rolls over. There's damp on the ceiling in here too, spilling in from the outside wall, and from her bed she can see rain on the window, a bit of next door's kitchen window and a corner of dark grey sky. She's been looking at this view all her life, every single summer. She remembers when they used to make her go to bed and it was still broad daylight and she could hear other kids playing on the shore. You need your sleep, Mum used to say, I'm not responsible for other people's children, but she kind of knew then and certainly knows now that they just wanted to get rid of her so they could – what, drink herbal tea, probably. Do crossword puzzles. The family renting next door have turned on the lights, which Mum would say is wasteful. All these long summer days, she says, even when it's cloudy the light lasts for ever, why would you want to blind yourself with the electric, don't we have enough artificial light all winter? Only so you can see, Becky thinks, only maybe if you find it fucking depressing fumbling round in the dark in a tiny wet cabin miles from anywhere when you could just as well be at home with normal-sized rooms and a downstairs loo as well as the bathroom so you don't have to be always smelling your brother's poo and normal internet access or at least data so you don't feel as if you've died. She wants to pick up her phone, even just to look at the photos, but there's no point.

I want to be dead.

They would be sorry, probably, though maybe Dad would just say she was stupid and crazy because he certainly wasn't sorry when she banged her head on the wall. She's tried cutting her wrists before, all the girls do, and it makes you feel better for a bit but you don't bleed anything like enough to die. Jamila took an overdose last year but then she had stomach pains and got scared and told her mum and they took her to hospital where everyone was angry with her and they pumped her stomach without giving her any sedatives or anaesthetic or whatever and made her drink this awful black gritty stuff and Jamila didn't even know if it was just a punishment or meant to make her better somehow. All I'm saying, she said, when Becky and Bridget were eventually allowed to see her afterwards, all I'm saying is next time I'll know not to tell anyone, either don't do it or follow through. And one of these days, Becky thinks, there's bleach under the sink, isn't there, knives in the drawer, though honestly based on past experience it would be pretty difficult to sever your own artery unless you were on drugs or something, high enough not to feel all the pain but not so high you couldn't actually do it. She's even got enough paracetamol in her handbag, for period pain she told Mum and she does sometimes take one for that but mostly it's just nice to know they're there, that if she feels like it she wouldn't even have to go to the shops where they won't sell you two packets at once in case you're suicidally organised enough to buy tablets but not so much it occurs to you to go to another shop for a second pack. Maybe if you were in some tiny village somewhere with only one shop and not even a petrol station it might work, but you'd probably have left or killed yourself years ago anyway.

Right. Fuck this. Becky wipes her nose on the back of

her hand and sits up. Lipstick. No point in anything else, it'd be all over her face by the time she even gets to the tent, but she rubs some serum through her hair and brushes it smooth, likes the smell. Her coat's by the front door so she takes Alex's hoody he's left lying on his bed, puts on her trainers, climbs over his bed – shoe print on the sheet, his own fault he didn't make it this morning – opens the window and drops out. The ledge hurts her thigh and her ankles jar; it's a much bigger drop outside than in but she doesn't specially want her parents to think that she's doing what they said and joining Alex at the pub after all and she's certainly not going to tell them where she is going.

It's still light, of course, as if this day will never bloody end, and still raining. She goes round the back of their cabin and picks her way over the grass behind next door, not that there's probably anyone watching, exactly, not that there's any reason she shouldn't be out, but that Eng-lishwoman with the baby has already tried to talk to her once, all patronising like a teacher. How are you finding your holidays, isn't the weather a pain, at least with the little ones we can play in the puddles but this can't be much fun for you. S'all right, Becky said, we're local, see, used to it. Fuck off back to England, then, if you don't like it here, she didn't say. Oh, I live here too, said the woman, well, Edinburgh, but I doubt the weather's much differ-ent, are you from Glasgow then? Aye, Becky said, frae

Glesga, right enough hen. There's a tile come off their roof and the rain running into the gap.

She'd better go round the back of the Ukrainians' lodge too, in case Mum's still looking out, though she'd like to see what's going on in there, the only people having any fun between Glasgow and fucking *Iceland*. She was lying awake listening all night, thinking she and Alex should just put their clothes back on and go round there, sounded like an excellent party and it's not as if anyone was getting any sleep anyway. Becky talked to the mum a bit, the first day they were here she went past and saw the woman was washing up with the kitchen window open talking to the little girl who was playing outside. It sounded a bit like Polish so Becky said 'dzień dobry' just to see if it worked. She'd learnt it at school when they had to make a big poster and say hello in the home language of everyone in her year and it turned out to be the same in basically every Eastern European country but it's not as if she's ever likely to have the chance to try it in any of them. The little girl stopped and stared at her and the mum was really surprised and put down her brush and leant so far out of the window her top went in the washing-up water, but of course Becky couldn't say anything else so the woman, Alina, had to speak English after all. Turned out she's Ukrainian, not Polish, and the first thing she said was she's been here twenty years and pays her taxes, as if Becky would care. She didn't invite Becky round. There are no lights on now, anyway, and Becky hasn't seen the little girl for a couple of days, she's maybe gone back to Glasgow with some of the visitors because it can't be any fun for her here. Well, it's no fun for anyone, is it? She pulls up her hood before all the serum washes out of her hair. Nothing's changing. The clouds aren't moving, it's not even getting dark, and there's no one else out. How would they know if there's some mass-extinction event in progress, how's that supposed to work with no phones?

She'll go round the front of the old people's cabin though she's no need to go down to the shore, just so she can walk across their view, not particularly fast. No hurry, is there? They're sitting in old-people chairs and they've each got one of those awful old-people dentist lights shining on books in their laps, as if they're about to do fillings rather than turn pages. Young people nowadays, she mutters, cluttering up our landscape in their horrible clothes, shoes like fridges. It's what her gran says, I don't know why you don't want to wear pretty shoes, when I was your age I was desperate for a pair of heels, I don't know how your dad can let you leave the house wearing those tights and nothing over your rear end, I wouldn't have stood for it. Becky stares in and yawns widely, not covering her mouth, and the old man looks up from his book and stares back. He looks as if he's on TV, she thinks, lit up like that behind the glass, as if the next thing is for someone to creep up behind him with a blunt instrument.

She goes along the side of the gravel track, not that anyone would hear her footsteps over the weather, past the cabin with the sad woman who never goes out and the two kids. They're still having their tea, and the scene reminds her of her old Playmobil dolls' house, the stiff-jointed figures you could arrange around a green plastic table, the tiny plastic cutlery Mum was always telling her not to lose. The rain is seeping through her leggings and Alex's hoody is beginning to cling to her hands at the cuffs. Maybe she'll take it off when she gets there, maybe she'll crawl into the soldier's tent and pull it and her T-shirt over her head in one smooth move and toss her hair – she practises tossing her hair though the hood is still up – and the soldier will seize her and they'll kiss, though actually he's old as well as weird and whatever they say about old men he's not shown any sign of want-ing to kiss her, but he's mostly interested in what she says and at least it makes a change from Mum and her banging on about recycling and sustainability and why they can't use cling film any more.

Becky reaches the road, where all the potholes are full of brown water, and sets off into the trees.

beginning to rise

Deep in the woods darkness is beginning to rise, gathering under wet branches and between heavy leaves. In their den, badgers uncurl, snuff the air, lumber into the evening. The vixen stirs and stretches out for her cubs to nurse. She's hungry, and when they're done – before the slow smallest one is done – she shakes off the runt, nudges them further into the dim warmth and gets to her feet.

The vixen threads the dusk, quick and low. The traces of small creatures have been washed away and there are no little birds on the wing. She snaffles a fat drowned slug, trots on. She knows a place for bacon rinds, stale baps, a chilly feast of fish skin and potato peel. As long as the cubs stay where she left them, as long as no hunting owl wings the night in her absence, as long as no late car strikes as she crosses the road, she will return and feed them again.

hold off your tornados

JOSH DOESN'T LIKE the weather. Well, of course he doesn't like the weather, he's not a masochist, unlike his mum he doesn't even secretly believe that rain is God's way of stopping Scots having sinful levels of fun. (He shouldn't be mean, though, didn't she after all hand over the keys knowing perfectly well that sinful levels of fun would be exactly what he had in mind and a whole year before the wedding, she'd have had some grief from her own mum about that.) But this time last year it was exactly twice as warm as it is now. He got sunburnt climbing the Ben. He was carrying a litre bottle of water everywhere. There were folk swimming all along the beaches. The water and sky were blue and he remembers spending about half an afternoon just sitting on a flat rock a couple of miles along the shore path watching the leaf-shadows on the sand and stones and the birds on the water, feeling as if his skin was photosynthesising sunlight. Felt good, right enough, but for the first time there were hosepipe bans even on the islands where people don't own hose-pipes, don't ordinarily want more water than the good Lord has already seen fit to pour on their leaking hoods and shoulder-seams. In some ways this year feels safer, as if being cold and wet makes climate change less bad than it was last year, but it's not right, this kind of downpour. It's as if the weather's got stuck, as if the whole arrangement, the Gulf Stream and the space winds, the water cycle itself, stuff we don't notice, has stopped. Won't the water be running out, somewhere else? There's only so much in the system.

He said he'd cook this evening, so he's flipping through the recipe book his mum keeps here though he knows fine well what he's going to make. Pasta surprise, they call it: couple of onions (sprouting a bit but that's OK, you can eat the greens), red pepper with the bit that's gone soft cut out, garlic also sprouting, wrinkly mushrooms but it won't matter once they're cooked, tin of tomatoes. It'll do the job but Milly's right, they really do need to go shopping tomorrow. He just likes it here with her, afternoon sex and morning sleep, the world centred around being in bed together, doesn't want to break the spell. They'll be back in the world soon enough, you probably don't get many days like this, days when love is your primary activity, in your whole life. Break the fishbowl more like, Milly said, break the bell jar, you know if we drove round to the station we could be in Glasgow in less than an hour, go to the Kelvingrove or the Women's Library, they've a festival on. She needs her friends, her tribe. It's not that he disapproves of women or libraries or festivals, any of that, he just doesn't want to go. It's not his thing, same way she doesn't want to go to the football, and they're supposed to be on holiday, doing things together. He missed the game at the weekend, didn't even mention it. The book's more photos than words. Roast lamb with apricots, which seems a strange idea and his mum never made any such thing, certainly not here where she tends to keep things simple, frozen pies and fish fingers because it's her holiday too, isn't it? Smoked haddock fishcakes, look a right faddle. Broccoli and stilton quiche, that's Milly's kind of thing. Though he's never made pastry and anyway they're out of eggs. We could go over to the pub, he says, if you fancy getting out, they do food.

Milly looks up, refocusing as if he's just pulled her from another horizon though he knows she's reading that book for the second time this week. I'm going to run out of proper books, she keeps saying, if you had wifi I could at least download e-books. *Proper books* means paper books, taking over their whole flat at home, piles starting to grow even in the kitchen. When they have their own place, on the island, he'll build shelves for her, all the shelves she could want. She shows him pictures, sometimes, in magazines, houses with shelves up the stairs and over the doors, nothing like any house he's ever been in, but he could do that, for her. The pub, she says, mm. What is there down the road, in the village? He shrugs. Another pub, he says. Not that I'm not happy to cook, I just thought if you wanted out— She's looking at the weather, at the rain dripping off the roof and the vagueness of the blotted loch behind the trees. Nah, she says, let's save the money and go out properly another night, somewhere good. There must be something maybe round the other side, on the main road. I looked at the menu in the pub here, we're better at home with pasta surprise.

He used to eat at the pub here with his mum and dad, for a treat.

She picks up her book again. She's curled up in his mum's chair like a cat, her feet tucked under. He remembers her earlier, laid out under him, the whole length of her his, her hair the brightest thing in the room. Later, maybe, again. Take her mind off things. He takes the onions out of the cupboard and decapitates them. He looks at her while she reads, while she won't see him admiring her and feel weird.

She's looking up. There's that girl, she says, the miserable one. Not that I wouldn't have been miserable, stuck here with my parents at her age.

He's chopping the pepper, noticing it bleeding into the scratches on his mum's white plastic chopping board. She's not really one for peppers, his mum. Meat and potatoes and a green vegetable and nothing wrong with that. Which girl, he says, to keep talking rather than because he thinks it's interesting when a girl walks across the park. Two cabins up, she says, her brother goes out in the red canoe. He shrugs. There are always kids here, messing around on the beaches. He and Kieran used to spend hours there when they were little, on the swing or just paddling and playing with the stones. He heard some kids playing down there earlier when he was bringing in the laundry Milly had so optimistically hung outside, some kind of war game, lots of shrieking. It's better for them, isn't it, than being inside playing war games on a screen? The kids on the island still play outside, all weathers. You know which girl, she says, mum in the hippy patchwork trousers? Don't know which dad, they all look the same, white bloke going grey, hiking boots, beige trousers with those awful zips. Vaguely, he says, though what he remembers is Milly talking about it. Some women, she said, just never got the memo when the second wave ended, where does she get those clothes, don't think I've ever seen patchwork dungarees in a shop. Feminism, he's learnt, has waves, though the tides seem very slow and there's time to write a lot of books Milly thinks he should have read in between each one. Simone de Beauvoir, he'd vaguely heard of her without knowing what it's all about, which was frankly just fine. Someone else, someone from now, he did read but didn't really understand, or at least didn't see how it was what he'd call feminist. He stirs the pepper. She'll be going to the pub, he says, would she not be too young? Milly's left her book and she's opening the door and craning her head round it. Cold air and the smell of rain blows through. She would and she's not, she says, looks to be going up the road. For phone signal, I suppose, must be missing her mates, she's going to get soaked with no coat on. Like you, he says, missing your mates, and she closes the door and comes over to him, stands behind him at the electric rings and puts her arms round his waist. Her breasts press soft against his back. She smells different here, the wrong shampoo or something. Nah, she says, I've got you, haven't I, not to mention I'm not fourteen. Poor girl.

At fourteen, they have agreed, they would not have liked each other. She was mostly into dance and he was mostly into weed. It's a good thing, really, they didn't meet any earlier. But she is missing her mates, he knows that, or at least missing her phone, missing the chorus of agreement and amusement and outrage that lives in it. He does wonder, sometimes, if the island is such a good idea, if she'd manage without the tribe who share and shore up her indignation with the version of the world they all inhabit. That's why she wants to go, a new beginning, clean air, learning to bake their own bread and see the stars and hear the birds, but he's not sure she's really understood that mostly the people who've always lived there aren't that interested in air pollution and sourdough and she's always liked thinking about birds and stars more than actually looking at them, here or at home. She buys books, tells her friends how birds have compasses in their minds, seem to be able to steer by the stars even though they fly during the day, how all the stars were named by men. She doesn't buy binoculars. Maybe she'll start a book group.

They could go out, there's a point four miles down the road where you get five bars' signal. Sometimes you see people sitting in their cars in the layby, refuelling on news and human contact, though Josh is finding that the longer he has no internet access, the less appetite he has for it. And when they drove down the road three days ago and his phone began to tremble and exclaim with his friends' past moods, it was like reading the weather forecast from last week. Unless there was a tornado or a tidal wave, unless there is a swathe of devastation still producing stories five days later, no one cares. And you can, he thinks, hold off your tornados and tidal waves as long as possible, thank you. No need to go looking, not just now, not while there's the two of them, here, warm and dry with a bed for sex and sleeping and a table and chairs for sharing food. Maybe that's all you need, really, a bed and a table. And bookshelves. People used to get by fine, didn't they, before sofas and all that, generations of his family on the island. Uncle Seumas's already offered him work, they'd have something, and Milly's right, the schools up there are often wanting teachers, she'd soon find something. You can get help, at the beginning, a young couple and especially once there are kids on the way, and she wants kids soon, she's always been clear about that. Look, she said, all of five months in, we'll see how this goes but just to save time, I'm not interested in a man who will never want kids. I like being with you but if you never want to be a dad, it's a matter of when not if we break up and it'll be easier all round to stop seeing each other now. Call me, she said, picking up her bag, if you want, and she left the pub, didn't even let him see her onto her bus. He called her before she got home. He can imagine her pregnant, the curves of her softened and swelling, more belly and more breast. It's hard to believe that he's really the one with whom her genes will pass down into the future. If there is a future; it's not as if having kids is looking like a kind or clever thing to do these days but you have to act as if there's hope, don't you? You can't plan your life around the end of the world. Mind out, he says – she's leaning her cheek on his shoulder – I just need to chop the mushrooms. Can I open some wine, she says, do you mind?

She needs it, he thinks, to get through the evenings here with him. He's not enough for her. How will they really manage, on the island? It's his dad who grew up there, Josh himself has always been a visitor, family right enough but it's not the same as living there. I love the community there, she says, the way everyone knows each other, the way there are old folk and the little ones at the ceilidhs, when do you ever see pensioners dancing with millennials in the city? And she's right, it's great, but what some would call the closeness of the community is also the challenge of living there. No privacy, nowhere to hide: the delivery guys know what you ordered online, the neighbours know when you went out and came home and probably also what time you turned out your bedroom light. Morag at the shop knows what kind of biscuits you like and how much beer you're buying and people don't say much, not to your face, but you know that they know. They know that you know that they know. He sometimes thinks maybe the visibility holds people to higher standards but his dad reckons they just get better at hiding and at shame, at seeing and not seeing. Not, his dad says, that it's not a good place to live, you just need a certain set of skills. A bit like here, really; Josh wonders if that's why Dad bought the lodge, to remind him of the watchfulness of home.

He hasn't answered but she's choosing a bottle, taking last night's glasses from the draining board. The mushrooms are too wizened to slice so he just hacks them a bit and chucks them in with the pepper. We're getting through it pretty quick, he says, was it two bottles last night in the end? She's pouring, red. Yeah, she says, but we started early. Mm, he says, just give me half for now.

She gives him a full glass and a dirty look, wanders back to the window, opens the door again. He sees her through the glass, sipping her wine on the deck as if the background was a holiday ad instead of the weather. He stirs the veg and then tips most of his own wine into the pan because the surprise is going to need all the help it can get.

She comes back in, wet footprints across the lino. There are raindrops in her hair. Even the little Russian girl's not out, she says, the one on her bike. Well, he says, you were worried when she was out the other night, you can't have it both ways. You know if we do have kids on the island, they'll be out in the rain? She shrugs, runs her fingers through the back of the new haircut which is fine but he liked it long, liked the way it took up space. I was concerned, she says, I wouldn't say worried, you barely see the mum all day and it didn't sound like a party for kids last night, did it, I did wonder where she was, there was a lot of drinking.

She's halfway down that glass already. Cheap shot. Nip over and introduce yourself, he says, maybe they'll invite us next time. If there's a next time I bloody will, she says, they were certainly having more fun than the rest of us, maybe that's what we should all be doing here in the rain, having parties, getting to know the neighbours. He fills the kettle. What, he says, him next door at a party, he hasn't been to a party since 1963. Anyway you were giving me the impression that you were having fun, actually. She comes back over to the stove, pokes at the veg and then pats his bum. Was I really, she says, well jolly good.

Imagine him, marrying someone who says *jolly good*, even ironically. Just as long as she doesn't say it to his mum. Or in the hearing of pretty much anyone in his family. He starts a pan of water; there isn't one that's big enough to do pasta properly here so it's going to be a bit gluey. Oh well.

She's over at the window again. Did you see the baby out earlier with his big sister and his dad, she says, he's so cute, he's just learning to walk, you know that stage when it's basically just not quite falling over? And they have this amazing confidence or drive or something, to keep getting up and trying again? When do we lose that, do you think, where does it go? He tries to remember if he's ever seen a baby learning to walk. I suppose they have to, he says, evolution wouldn't favour someone who fell over and just packed in the whole walking idea. Mothers would, though, she says. You wouldn't just leave your baby lying there for the next woolly mammoth. I don't think woolly mammoths eat babies, he says, wondering what on earth they're talking about. She wanders across the room, picks up one of Mum's china swan ornaments from the sideboard, turns it over. Just put your coat on and go for a walk, he thinks. Borrow a kayak. Do some of your yoga. He likes watching her do yoga, the seriousness of her face, the way she moves. You can tell she used to dance. She puts the swan down and goes back to the window. It's still not getting dark out there. Do you think everyone else is looking out of their windows too, she says, do you think we're all watching the rain? He stirs his veg, adds the garlic – took him years to learn not to put it in until the other stuff's nearly cooked – hopes a tin of the good Italian tomatoes will save the day. Maybe they're all having sex, he says, maybe they're all taking excellent drugs. Before the party. Sit down, he says, put your feet up, let me bring you some of those nuts and your maga-zine. I've hardly had my feet down today, she says, tomorrow we'll go out, yes, whatever the weather? Sure, he says, of course, we need food anyway. Tomorrow, I promise. And they will, he thinks, drive down past the scattered houses to the village but she'll want to go on to the town where the trains bring the scent of the city, and where there's a proper supermarket whose strip lighting will shine on the tenderness of these last few days and erase it, whose shoppers will notice the lift of her hair and the shape of her in her jeans and her amazing eyelashes. Which is all fine, of course, they can't hide here for ever, he knows that. He does.

flights begin

Bats rouse earlier on these grey days. All day they have been hanging from the rafters of the old barn like pears on a tree. The first one flaps into wakefulness and then there's an outbreak of life, an explosion of fluttering. Utterances too high for human hearing pierce the air, bounce off the old stone walls and the undersides of the slate roof. Flights begin, fast as falling, but as the bats start to trickle out into the dimming sky, their high notes are returned by raindrops. Midges will blossom when the rain stops. Moths will turn to the moon when the clouds clear, but for now, there is nothing to eat.

shadow people

IZZIE CAN'T SLEEP. Daddy came and said good night to her hours and hours ago and then she heard them putting Pat to bed, which isn't fair because he's four and a half years younger than her. Mum sang the song she used to sing for Izzie, hó-bhan, hó-bhan, Goiridh òg O, I lost my darling baby-o. I saw the trace of the swan on the lake, but not a sign of baby-o. But Mum didn't add Izzie's special verse about *finding* the darling baby-o which means that in Izzie's mind and maybe in Pat's dreams the baby is still lost, lying out there beyond the track of the wee brown otter and the mountain mist. There's still talking through the wall but it's starting to get dark outside and soon they'll go to bed too and Izzie will be the only person awake, the only one to know if a bad thing happens, and it almost is a bad thing, when the grown-ups go to sleep, especially with the doors shut. She didn't mind at first, when it was still light. I'm just closing it so we don't disturb you, Daddy said, sleep tight, be bright, night night gorgeous girl.

SARAH MOSS

Izzie pushes back the duvet, which is too hot anyway, kneels up on the bed and unhooks the cord for the blind. You can't leave cords dangling because babies put their heads through them and die, but Izzie knows how to undo it and wind it back up again so that if Pat comes in here and somehow gets onto her bed he can't die, or at least not from the cord although he could still fall off and bang his head. Babies have big heads and weak necks so you have to be very careful with a baby's head. She tries the wrong cord first, makes the blind tilt instead, and then pulls gently and steadily so it slides up, and the strips rattle a little but with the door closed Mummy and Daddy won't hear. She doesn't want it too far up, not so that someone outside would think it was open, or see her looking out, because there are people outside. There's the big girl from the cabin next door who stays up much later than Izzie, a girl who's allowed to scuffle about on her pink bike with streamers some days until it's properly dark and sometimes she sees Izzie and waves and smiles, but she probably won't be out in this rain. But there's someone else, in the woods, someone who comes most days and stands in the shadows at dusk. He sometimes seems to look this way but Izzie always ducks and she doesn't think he's seen her.

She sits back on her heels and rests her chin on her hands on the windowsill, so that her eyes are level with the opening. He's not there yet. She can't remember, does he maybe not come in the rain? Or is he sheltering, under

168

the trees? She puts her eyes right up to the window, presses her forehead against it. The raindrops go blurry and she blinks. There's mist on the window now and she draws a flower on it with her finger, four big petals and then a little one because she's run out of room. When she's bigger she wants a pink bike with streamers. She wants shiny patent shoes and white lacy tights like that girl. She puts her fingertip against a new raindrop and traces its path down the glass. Raindrops don't go straight down, ever. They go round each other sometimes, like magnets that won't touch. Another one. She tries to do two at once, with the forefingers of each hand, but you can't watch them well enough to get it right. One at a time. He's still not there, the tree man.

Izzie folds her fingers the way Granny showed her. Here is a church, here is a steeple, open the doors, here are the people. She doesn't think she's been in a church, but there is one, with a steeple, by the bus stop at home. Suddenly she needs to be there, at home, with her butterfly wallpaper and pink curtains, in her own bed with all her toys and knowing that Maddie upstairs is in her bed on the other side of the ceiling. She doesn't like it here at night, there are no streetlights to come on and if she wakes up later it will be thick, woolly dark, the sort of dark that fills up your mouth when you open it so you can't call out as well as not being able to see, so that whatever came at you with bony fingers there would be nothing you could do – Izzie wants to get out of bed and go find Daddy, but now she's scared to move because of the dark place under the bed which is exactly the right size for a crawling snatching thing with long arms, like a giant spider, scuttling, but with pincers. She tips over and squirms under the duvet and curls up small with it over her head, but it's still not her own bed or her own duvet and she has only Elsie Bear to hold because Mummy left all the others at home, and what if there's a fire or burglars there while they're away, what if all her bed toys are being stuffed into a sack and taken away so they'll never see her again, or if they're burning, if their whole flat is burning, and Maddie's flat too because they're joined together? What if Maddie's burning? There's no air under this duvet.

Izzie comes up. It's darker than it was, dusk gathering by the door and under the dressing table and especially in the mirror. She tries to look away from the mirror. There isn't one in her room at home and she hadn't realised that they're scary, especially in the dark, that things seem to move in them. She keeps forgetting that the mirror isn't a window, that there isn't another room on the other side of it, another dark room with another door through which shadow people could come, all the dead people who live underground. She looks at the real window, where light is now reaching in through her peephole, but she doesn't feel safe turning her back to the room and the mirror-room to see out. How can you be sure, in the dark, which is the window and which the mirror? He's probably there now, the tree man, in one or the other. She hears Mummy laughing in the living room, and then Daddy's voice, and that gives her courage to sit up and wrap the duvet firmly around her shoulders and kneel again at the window, offer the back of her head to the mirror. It's still raining and the clouds are a funny colour, but there's enough light yet for Izzie to see the shadow cast from the kitchen window, where the grown-ups have the light on now, and to see across the fading grass to the nearest trees.

There is someone moving, someone coming round the house, too close, creeping, but just while Izzie's trying to find her voice to call Daddy the figure goes past and turns into the red boat boy's sister, wearing the red boat boy's top with the hood up and her hair hanging over her face, and while Izzie's watching she goes round the back of her own cabin and kind of scrabbles at the wall and then she's in through the window and Izzie's wondering if that counts as a burglar, if someone's breaking in to her own house, though she didn't break anything. She watches while the light comes on, a square of light making a square of bright raindrops in the dark, and then she remembers to look for the tree man.

She was right, he is there, in the trees. Just standing, watching.

From out of sight, the music begins to play.

maybe they dream

The trees change shape at night. In the darkness, limbs relax, leaves droop. Branches reach out for each other, like holding hands. It's tiring, raising boughs to the sun, making energy of sunlight. Come night the trees' bodies have less work. The pressure in their cells falls a little, like ours. Like us, like any creature, they don't stop at night. Some tree-mind keeps the respiration running, tends the flow of sap. Some green thought reads the turning of the earth and the slow tilt towards winter.

The woods expand, settle down for the night, offer a little more shelter to those who need it. Trees sleep, more or less. Maybe some nights they dream and wake, check the darkness, sleep again till dawn.

a woman sitting on the edge

HE'S NOT BEING racist. Even though they weren't meant to be here any more, it's no odds to him that they're foreign, Romanian or what have you. He'd feel just the same about a bunch of lads from Stockport, and in fact he did feel the same and said so, that time they went to Scarborough and there was a stag party in the upstairs flat, and he doesn't see why just because this lot is Bulgarian or whatever he should treat them any differently. It's not OK, is it, keeping dozens of people up all night, they should have some consideration, there are young families here and old folk not to mention Justine was up at silly o'clock running, her own choice maybe but she doesn't ruin everyone else's sleep just because she likes to be up at unsocial hours. Live and let live, that's what Steve thinks. They can stay up all night and deafen themselves if they want to but they should do it somewhere else, such as back where they came from. A holiday park in the middle of the summer break, for Pete's sake.

He can feel the bass coming through the ground, echoing around the crawl space between the earth and the floorboards, vibrating in his bones. Christ, he says, someone should really say something to that lot. Justine sighs, pauses whatever she's watching on her laptop and takes out an earbud. On the screen, he can see a woman frozen with her red lipsticked mouth open and a glass of wine in midair. He wishes he'd thought to download something of his own to watch. What, she says. I said, he says, someone should say something. About that racket. We can't have it going on all bloody night again, it's ruining the whole bloody holiday, everyone shattered all the time. Yeah, she says, it is a bit loud, and she puts her earbud back and presses play.

He pushes himself up out of his chair – she's not wrong, Justine, he should do more exercise – and goes to tell the boys it's OK, he's going to deal with it, they'll get their sleep, but when he pushes their door open over the weird thick carpet, they both seem to be asleep, or at least are lying motionless in the darkening room although the sound – almost more like force than sound, something you feel in your bones more than your ears – is pulsing through the windows and the wooden walls. Is the music bothering you, he whispers, I'll go make them turn it down. Noah turns over and looks at him, confused. What, he says, I was nearly asleep. Shh, says Steve, go back to sleep then, I was just worried that music would keep you up. Oh, says Noah, no Dad, it's all right, and he lies down again.

Steve goes into the bathroom to see how loud it is there. Loud, is the answer. He thinks the bass is making ripples in the water in the toilet bowl, echoing in the empty bathtub. His head is starting to ache, a hard weight in the base of his skull. He rubs his neck, catches sight of the movement in the mirror over the basin. It feels as if there's one of those round stones from the beach lodged in there, and his reflection looks pale, uneasy, the face of a man who didn't expect to be caught. Maybe it's a brain tumour, don't they start with headaches? Maybe he's going to die, maybe that's why he's been so tired recently, not, as Justine likes to imply, too many bacon sarnies and not enough running but a tragic disease striking him down in his prime. Well, *prime* might be pushing it. You probably don't notice when you're in your prime, do you; in fact, if you're thinking about your prime it's almost certainly over. He catches his eye again. Mirrors are weird in the dark, everyone knows that. He picks up the bathmat which the boys have left damp on the floor, hangs it over the towel rail, flushes the loo which for some reason Eddie doesn't, ever. The song changes, something faster with yipping and caterwauling pouring through the trees and still that bass like a boy bouncing a ball against the wall. It must be going right out over the water, the fish in the loch must be hearing it, scaring birds out of their nests and probably even keeping the damn sheep awake. Don't sheep lose their lambs if they get distressed? He'd be doing something for the local farmers, too, if he went round there and told those Bulgarians what's what.

He goes back down the hall to the kitchen. He fills the kettle in the dusk; you can still see what you're doing, just about. Justine's face glows in the dim room, up-lit by her screen. He's not the only one starting to show his age, all the running and yoga in the world won't undo the way her neck and chin are beginning to droop or the scribbled lines suddenly marked under her eyes. We're halfway through, he thinks, not a new thought, exactly, a man knows when he turns forty, but he hasn't really thought about Justine ageing before, that one day she might be holding on to his arm the way her mum does, will want him to carry the bags and do all the driving. Will she? Her mum's always been a bit like that, a bit lame, though she's a good cook, better than Justine, and keeps a cleaner house. Justine's probably still going to be lifting weights in her nineties, isn't she, years past the point where normal people have decided they've already beaten the odds and can eat all the pies and drink all the beer they can lift because they're not going to ask your bloody cancer risk at the golden gates, are they? Maybe it won't be so bad, ageing. He drops a couple of teabags into the pot. The thing is, it's all downhill from here, which is a daft thing to say because it's not as if people in their thirties are getting younger either, look at it that way and it's all downhill from birth, death approaching minute by passing minute, kids too, but he knows what he means. It's different, being past the midpoint. It just is. The young are younger and the older not so old.

He pours the boiling water, watching the steam rise and drift on the darkening air. He glances up again at his wife, who is biting the skin off the sides of her fingernails, grimacing and baring her teeth as if he isn't even here. Even with the earbuds, she must be able to hear the noise, must know that someone has decided that everyone within about a three-mile radius is just going to have to listen to their racket, that one Romanian gets to decide what every other soul has to hear for hours and hours of the night, that one person's urge to party trumps everyone else's need to sleep. He'll go round there, he thinks, and kill them with his bare hands, he'll kick the door in, he'll rip the speakers from the wall and throw them through the bloody windows, that's what he'll do. And then there will be peace.

Do you want a cup of tea, he says to Justine, but she's too busy with her box set and her fingernails to respond. He goes over and taps her shoulder: on screen, there's a woman sitting on the edge of a shiny kitchen counter in a puffy red dress with her white knees wide open, bracing her arms behind her while a man in a suit appears to be giving her oral sex under the skirt. Justine pauses it again and takes out an earbud. Now what, she says. I said, he says, do you want a cup of tea. No thanks, she says, and she waits, frowning, until he's back in the kitchen before she restarts the action. What the hell is she watching? It's typical, isn't it, when a man watches porn he's dirty and dangerous and it's degrading to women but she can just sit there on the sofa for all the world to see, getting all hot and bothered over her laptop. Her work laptop, he might add, property of her employer. She could get sacked for that and then where'd they be, not as if they could manage on what he earns, not these days. The song's changed again, a surging, rolling beat against an angry male voice. You can't really hear the words but he'd bet good money they're not what you'd want your kids to say. Do they have rap in Poland? He pours himself tea, takes the last of the milk which means there won't be any for breakfast not that there was enough anyway, adds two heaped spoons of sugar and leaves the spoon on the counter, sticky. Is that what she wants, to sit on the counter like that? Is that what he needs to do to get some action these days? How does it even work, how could you get your mouth where it needs to be if she's parked her backside on a hard surface, wouldn't your chin get in the way? It doesn't make sense, fucking American films with their acres of kitchen and fridges the size of cars. They probably have a special counter insert for the purpose, along with their ice-dispensers and garbage-disposal units and what have you.

Who wears a big dress like that in real life anyway, especially in the kitchen? Oh fucking hell, they've just turned the music up even louder. There ought to be built-in limits on those things, like the speed limiters on goods vehicles, not that people wouldn't find a way to disable them. Bloody Bulgarians.

He takes his tea over to the French windows, carefully going round the front of Justine and her work laptop. The first day they were here, he watched the sunset at just about this time. It goes down behind the mountains of course, you'd need to be over on the west coast for the whole thing, but the clouds went mad shades of neon pink and the sky was a deeper and deeper blue, almost unnatural colours, and later when he got up to pee he noticed the stars and went out on the deck to look, and it was just him standing there under the night sky with more stars than he'd ever seen in his life and the water reflecting a quarter-moon and he thought, bloody hell, this is me, then, and this is space, kind of wanted to go down to the beach but it was proper cold and him in his pants and T-shirt, plus it felt a bit funny, woods in the dark, so he just stood there and watched the stars until the cold got to him.

There's no sunset today. Rain runs down the windows and drips from the roof, and in the window there's the reflection of Justine's laptop hanging in a wet tree. It's all going black and white; when Steve was little he thought all the colours left at night, and he still doesn't really see that that's not true. How does anyone know there are colours in the dark, it's not as if you can see them. There are patches of yellow light coming from most of the other cabins, and two doors along he can just see the Romanians, their windows open despite the weather and someone standing in the open door, smoking. Unless they own that cabin, and he very much doubts they do, there's no smoking allowed here and he'd have thought any idiot could see why smoking in a wooden cabin in a wood ten miles up a single-track road was a bad idea, even if you're not bothered about lung cancer and heart disease and all that. And what about the little girl, passive smoking? He's old enough to remember all that, what it was like to be a kid in the back of a car with someone puffing away in the front, and also the way your clothes and hair used to stink after getting the bus with all the smokers in the back seat, as if that made any difference. He might not run all the time, might like the odd night down the pub and sugar in his tea, but at least Steve knows better than that. Never had a cigarette in his life, actually; after watching his mum nurse his grandad he wasn't that stupid, and if he ever catches Noah or Eddie at it he'll bloody murder them.

Why's the daft cow standing in the door like that, just to make sure no one can miss a single yell and thud of her so-called music? Must be catching her death of cold and getting wet into the bargain, and with those windows open there'll be rain getting onto the carpets. If he knew who owned the cabin, he'd be on the phone right now. Well, not right now, obviously, you can't call from here, but he'd go up the road or out on the jetty even to let them know what's going on, never mind the weather. It's not right, to rent someone's cabin that they've worked and saved for and then stink it out with cigarettes and ruin the carpet with rain and God knows what else they'll be up to in there, filthy it is, probably, people like that. He drinks some tea. Maybe he will go round there. Who else is going to deal with it, the old bloke with the doddery wife? There's the chap two doors along with the teenage son who was out in his kayak earlier, maybe Steve will call on him and they can go round together. Show the Bulgarians they're pissing off everyone, not just one grumpy bloke. That lad could come too, he's tall, towers over his dad. If they don't turn that noise down in the next five minutes, Steve's going to put his coat on.

Justine's still staring at her laptop. God knows what's going on there now, pervy shit he doesn't even want to think about, she's probably got that red dress off by now and maybe it's her turn to kneel on her polished kitchen floor between the polished shoes of the man in the suit, not that that would be doing it for Justine, she's never been— The Romanian woman's taking out her phone now, he can see her face in its blue glow. Classy, fag in one hand, phone in the other. You can kind of see her cleavage too, and bits of a dark bra showing over her top. She won't be calling anyone, that's for sure, couldn't make herself heard if she tried, but she's not, just fiddling with it, swiping and tapping, messaging her dealer he'd think if they weren't all the way out here. Wait, he thinks, how come she has reception? What's she doing, must be on a different network but everyone has to go up the road or onto the jetty for two bars, whoever they're with. Unless there's some Romanian provider with better coverage, but that doesn't make any sense, certainly not how it used to work, before. He can see her smiling, fat cow, and dark hair falling into those hoiked-up tits. Justine had long hair when they met and for years afterwards, until she got it all cut off so it was quicker to wash after running, didn't even tell him she was going to do it. It's her hair, of course, he knows that, but you'd think she might care what her husband likes. He'd ask her, if he wanted to grow a beard or shave his head or something. Not that he's the type and that's one thing at least, he's not going bald yet, or barely, not like his dad who had this terrible comb-over that used to lift in a strong wind. Steve knows how to face facts better than that.

Headlights sweep the trees, make him jump. Of course he wouldn't have heard an engine, would he, they could probably be breaking the sound barrier overhead and no one would notice. That used to happen up on the moors near home, before, when there were the Air Force bases up to the north, used to be exciting, the way the fighter jets would rip the sky and you'd look up and they'd be ninety degrees ahead of where you heard them. He'd have liked to go in one of those. It's big, whatever it is, and here it comes, lurching and swaying, looks like one of those new Sasquatch Adventurers, white and shiny as ice and bloody hell it's only stopping at the fucking Romanians' place. Justine, he says, would you just come and look at this, but of course she doesn't respond. There's other music coming from the car as soon as they open the doors, two sets of drums now banging against each other, two voices howling. The engine stops and people get out, two men from the front and from the back two women in white trainers you can see in the dark and tight little pale dresses, and the men go round and get what look like boxes of beer out of the boot while the fat cow with the phone comes right out into the rain to hug the women and then the little girl appears in the doorway and all the time the music's howling and thudding. Fucking hell, Steve thinks, we're going to need a whole bloody army now.

drums

The sound waves pulse like the rings around a thrown stone, spreading out across the rainy night.

Music crosses raindrops, the air full of noises and riddled with movement. Sound waves travel through the cabin's open door and through the gaps in the windows, over the waterlogged earth, into all the ears in the woodland. The fox cubs feel it through the earth of their den, the bats in their rafters. In a nest of bracken up on the hillside, the doe pricks her ears towards a running beat too heavy for wolves. The anthill pulses. Damp trees absorb the higher frequencies, swallow the energy into the wetness and wood-flesh, so it is the bass that penetrates your head and drums on the drums inside.

noise in his body

MUM AND DAD don't like it when he gets out of bed after they've turned off the light, but Jack's been lying here awake for hours, all the time it was still light, watching darkness seep up the walls. They must know he can't sleep through that noise and anyway he's thirsty, he needs a drink of water. He can feel the drumming in his bed, coming through the mattress into his bones, and the singer, the shouter, coming over the air through the glass and into his ears, deep into his head. They're playing on him, he thinks, they're making a noise inside his body and he can't stop them. He can't get away, and he's out of bed, out of the room. It's dark in the hall, the lino cold on his feet and the whole floor shuddering to the music's beat. Dad, he says, Dad. There's a line of yellow light under the door to the main room. In here, says Dad, and his voice makes a little space in the noise. What's up, says Dad, can't sleep? He's sitting in one of the big chairs, a green bottle of beer at his side, and he's just paused something on the

TV, two men talking over an open car door somewhere grey and rainy. Jack eyes him. Usually you need a reason to be out of bed, toilet's best, no one can object. It's so loud, he says. Yeah, says Dad, your mum's been complaining too. Lola asleep? Jack shrugs. We've not been talking, he says. Even when they're sharing a bedroom on holiday, they're supposed to lie quietly and go to sleep when Dad turns out the light. They might not need the rest but Mum does.

The song ends and they both pause like the men on the television. The music starts again, a gathering of notes before the violence of the bass.

Dad grunts as he stands up. Go pee, he says, have a drink of water and then go back to your bed. I'll deal with this, I'll just check on Lola first.

Jack follows Dad down the hall and hears Lola's voice as he goes into the bathroom, which is full of steam that smells like Grandad's roses in summer, too much. Mum must have just had a bath. He manages a bit of pee, holding the seat up because it doesn't stay, washes his hands with the weird-smelling soap they have here and then scoops a few mouthfuls of soapy-tasting water. The music pounds through the cabin. When he comes out, Mum's standing there in her dressing gown and Lola's out of bed too, talking to Dad by the door. Isn't it horrible, says Mum, they've no consideration, all last night was bad enough but now again, we can't stay here if we're never to get any sleep, I can't bear it and this was meant to be our holiday. All that money. Ian, I'm so tired. I'll sort it, Dad says, go to bed love, you'll get your rest. Mum's always tired. Sometimes she's so tired she cries. Please, Lola says, let me come too, maybe if they see you have a little girl they'll be nicer. Dad looks at Lola. He looks out of the window. There are more of them, he says, another car just arrived. All right then. But the moment I tell you to come back here, you do it, understood? She nods. Lola always gets Dad to do what she wants. Lola always does what Dad tells her, at least while he's watching. Ian, says Mum, are you sure? Dad's fastening his coat. Keep things civil, he says, I'll ask nicely first, I'm not going looking for trouble, and if not she'll be back here in ten seconds. You can watch her all the way. We can't have this, look at the state of you. Put your coat on, Lola.

Jack watches. Just little girls, then. Not that he wants to go, not if there's going to be shouting. Lola's got something in her coat pocket, something she's touching. She's biting on a small smile. Maybe one of the stones from the beach. He doesn't like remembering that, the girl. Violetta. Anyway someone needs to stay with Mum, who's looking as if she might cry again. You have to give her a hug and bring her tissues and if she can't stop, make her a cup of tea. Sometimes it goes on for a long time. Some days she just stays in bed and cries until Dad comes home and Jack has to make eggs or beans on toast for tea. He's good at frying eggs now, doesn't break the yolks. But Dad and Lola aren't going to be a long time. He looks out of the window and sees the dad from the cabin below looking out of his window, and over the way the little kids' mum standing on her deck. Everyone's watching, he says.

He can feel the beat in his feet, coming through the floor. Above the dance music, a bird calls. Not an owl, Jack thinks, a daytime bird. Its nest must be shaking like the cabins. I'm so tired, it's saying, I can't stay here if there's no rest. What's Dad going to say to them, to the Shit-chenkos? Bloody typical, Dad says, look out there, faces in half the windows and everyone watching and waiting for someone else to say something. The state of this country. Come on, Lola, we'll show them how you handle yourself. Lola smiles up at Dad and takes his hand.

Rain blows in when Dad opens the door and Mum says, oh, it's so cold, and she'll get wet, she's only wearing her pyjamas under that coat, but the door's closed before she's finished. You can't really listen to Mum, is the problem, or everything turns into a worry, but then she worries because nobody's listening to her. Jack thinks about what Dad would say to her, or at least what Dad would say on a good day. It's only a step, he says, Lola won't melt and she'll soon warm up when she's back in bed. I suppose so, says Mum, are they going in?

Jack goes right up to the window and cups his hands around his face to shut out the reflection of the kitchen light and Mum's un-made-up face over her dressing gown. They're standing at the door talking, he says, and his breath mists the window. A line of light opens across the grass, catching raindrops in flight, and he sees the neighbouring dad coming up the path. He opens his mouth to tell Mum and closes it again; some things don't alarm her but if you don't tell her anything you don't have to worry about which ones they are. He can feel his stomach twisting again, the ache starting up. The other dad isn't going fast, but Dad and Lola are still on the Shit-chenkos' deck when he comes up behind them. Dad's not shouting, Jack's pretty sure, even though he can see only his back, and Lola's standing a bit behind with her toes turned out. Second position; Lola's good at ballet. The Shit-chenko woman steps back into the cabin and a man comes out with two bottles dangling from between his fingers and nods and hands one to Dad and one to the other dad, and then all of them go inside.

The music plays on and Jack looks at the place on the doorstep where they were.

What's happening, says Mum, why is it still so loud? She seems to have got stuck in the doorway from the hall, as if she's too scared of the noise to come any closer. It reminds Jack of when you try to feed a squirrel in the park and you and the squirrel both know it wants the bread but you also both know it doesn't trust you enough to take the crust out of your hand. They've all gone in, he says, Dad's having a beer, why don't you go back to bed, I'm sure they'll turn it down soon. Oh, she says, I don't know, why can't he just come back here, what about Lola? She went in too, says Jack, and the dad from two doors down, you know, the one with the little boys, red car. Mum nods. The mum's the skinny woman who runs, she says, out there on her own, she's brave, I'll give her that. Oh, give over, Dad would say, everyone's bloody brave compared to you. Yes, Jack says, him. Oh, says Mum.

The music plays on. Jack thinks he's almost starting to like it, that it will be weird when it finishes, like when you get out of a car after a long journey and after the first few steps you realise that you miss hearing the engine, feeling it in your bones. He leans against the wall and feels the drums along his back. He lets his head bob a bit, to the beat. Maybe Lola's dancing in there, doing one of her routines. With the Shit-chenkos.

I'm so tired, Mum says again. Are they coming out yet? Jack shakes his head. Go lie down, Mum, he says. I'll keep watching and I'll tell you if anything happens. Mum sags. All right, she says, thanks love. You'll call me if you need anything? Jack can't imagine that he'll need anything or that he'd call her if he did. Yeah, course, he says.

Once her footsteps have shuffled down the hall, he turns off the light, holding the switch down so it doesn't click. Darkness expands around him, the hollows and corners spilling over, and he stands still, waits for the room to reassemble itself as his eyes adapt. A little red light on the fridge he hadn't noticed before is staring at him; he turns his back to it but it's still there. It's easier to see out of the window without the reflection. Next door's door stays closed but through the window he can see a woman reaching up to put her arms around a man's neck, a bottle still in one hand, and their bodies moving together. The woman dances away from the man, arms raised, bottom twitching from side to side, still waving that bottle, and back so the two shapes merge again. Jack glances round and then tries it himself, hands over his head, hips moving, here beside the wet coats on their hooks and the scratched steel draining board. He moves his head, his shoulders. It feels good. The music goes through his bones, fills his head and pulses away the pain in his belly. He dances back to the window, where he sees the young couple who never open the curtains before lunchtime if you know what I mean, barely left the park all week, coming hand in hand by the light of the woman's phone towards Violetta's cabin. The man's carrying a bottle of wine. Jack stops dancing. They're all going, he thinks, everyone's going to the party, and for a moment he imagines what would happen if he said, Mum, come on, let's go over there too, let's take Dad's whisky and go dancing.

The couple who don't open their curtains knock at the door, but of course no one can hear them so the woman just opens it, leans in, and one of the men from the car comes and takes the bottle, kisses her cheek and lets them both in. He can hear laughing and shouting as well as the music. He's never been to a party for grown-ups. What can Dad be doing there, he doesn't really laugh and you can't imagine him dancing. Dad wouldn't like it if Jack turned up, not that you can leave Mum on her own. He raises his arms again, dances back across the room to his own ghostly reflection in the French windows, nods and wiggles at himself. He bends back and shimmies his hips, comes back up, jumps and spins, pumps his arms.

And the dancing around the room, he'll think later, later and often, was why he didn't see the flames sooner. The dancing was why he didn't notice when the laughing stopped and the shouting sounded different.

The dancing was why by the time he'd smelt the smoke and gone to look and rushed back to pull the fire extinguisher from its holder on the wall – surprisingly difficult, that – and run barefoot over the wet grass and checked the diagram by the flickering light already coming from the Shit-chenkos' window and pulled the part you pull and pushed the part you push, it was too late.

And the dancing was why by the time he shouted and ran and banged on the doors of the people who weren't at the party, on the door where the skinny brave woman was in the house with her kids and the door of the posh old guy with the doddery wife and the door of the older boy with the red boat and his grumpy sister who never puts a coat on even in this weather, and they all came out and then went back for their fire extinguishers and came back again, running, even the old man, already the flames were shining on the branches and the daytime birds thought it was morning.

The dancing was why the fire had time to take hold so that Dad and Lola and the other dad had to climb out of the bathroom window of the burning cabin and the neighbours fired their fire extinguishers and brought wet towels and buckets of water, and the boy with the red boat went in, right into the flaming building because the fire brigade had been called by then, by the skinny running woman who ran to the pub, but the wooden building was going fast, faster than you'd expect really given the weather, and everyone knew how far the fire engine had to come, how long you'd be able to see the blue flashes signalling off the water and through the trees before help arrived.

The men from the car came out from the back of the burning cabin, one of them half-carrying the other whose feet didn't seem to be working, and the old man and the boat boy's dad ran over to them and laid the foot-dragging man on the ground, on the wet grass and the leaves, and turned him on his side and the other man bent over and threw up, right there in front of everyone, stuff dripping out of his mouth and pooling by his feet in the firelight, and no one paid any attention.

A tall bearded man in an Army jacket came out from the trees carrying an axe, a real axe glinting in the flames, and Jack thought for a moment that he was part of the fire somehow, that now the killers and creepers Lola talked about at night were coming out of the wood, but when the man raised the axe he started hacking at the burning window frame where the boat boy had gone in, and Mum was there, outside, not stopping in the doorway but running and shouting for Lola who stayed where she was, watching. Mum brought the running woman's kids and the mum and baby and toddler from over the way into the kitchen, talking to them, to people she'd never even met before, saying, you come in here, it's not for kids to be watching, this, you stay here in the warm, and the baby was crying but no one was doing anything about it and Jack stood there, quiet in the corner. Come on, Jack, Mum said, help me, and he went to help but she was moving really fast, she pulled the duvets from the beds, hauled them off herself and carried them bundled in her arms out into the rain to put over the people lying on the ground and Jack followed her but only as far as the steps. The curtain couple were out again and they looked weird by now, their faces dark and their eyes too white. He stood there breathing smoke and feeling the heat on his face and arms and watched Mum use his duvet, his duvet from home, to put over one of the women from the big shiny car when the red boat boy brought her over and she was crawling on the ground and sicking up white froth, the fire louder now, growling, and Mum tried to get the young couple to stop, to come in and have a drink, but they wouldn't because where was the little girl, where was the little girl with the shiny shoes and the bicycle, and where was her mum? The curtain couple and the boat boy tried to go back, right into the flames, although the boat boy's dad was telling him not to, because there was still the little girl in there, wasn't there, the little girl and her mum, weren't they still inside? The other little girl, not Lola. Lola was still standing there, watching, her hand in her pocket, her smudged face and her hair pale in the firelight.

Violetta, Jack said, though no one was listening to him, her name's Violetta, the other little girl.

The axe man chopped at the wall again and the boat boy and the curtain couple held red-checked tea towels on their faces and the old man knelt on the ground next to the woman wrapped in Jack's duvet. His Batman duvet cover was on the ground, wet and muddy round a woman he'd never seen before and her mouth looked as if she was making a noise but you couldn't hear it over the music and the fire.

The flames were too big. The curtain man pulled the curtain woman and the boat boy back from the burning walls, and then there was a bit where everyone waited, stood back like on Bonfire Night and the music was still playing, the beat still coming through the noise of the flames.

And then the music did stop and then there came a human sound he never wants to hear again and will always be hearing, somewhere in his head, and he was right, Jack, you notice, when it stops.

Acknowledgements

This book began one wet summer in Scotland. I thank my family for believing that there's no such thing as bad weather.

I thank my brilliant and dedicated editor, Kish Widyaratna; Camilla Elworthy and everyone at Picador in London; Jenna Johnson and the team at Farrar, Straus and Giroux in New York; Anna Webber at United Agents for afternoon teas in the face of interesting times as well as superb representation and Seren Adams for second readings.

Sinéad Mooney was, as always, my first reader, and as always she was right. I thank the MacDonald-Badenoch clan for advice on titles and terms, and especially Helen MacDonald for her ear for Scottish teenagers. Thank you to Asher Kaboth for answering questions about sound-waves and wet trees, to TM for expertise on fox cubs and the dream life of deer. All errors of fact or probability remain my own.

Also by
Sarah Moss

THE FELL

Published November 2021

**From the *Sunday Times* bestselling author of
Summerwater, *The Fell* is a novel for our times – the story
of a woman in quarantine who can't take it any longer and
leaves home to go hill-walking . . .**

At dusk on a November evening in 2020 a woman slips out
of her garden gate and turns up the hill. Kate is in the middle
of a two week quarantine period, but she just can't take it
anymore – the closeness of the air in her small house, the
confinement. And anyway, the moor will be deserted at
this time. Nobody need ever know.

But Kate's neighbour Alice sees her leaving and Matt, Kate's son,
soon realizes she's missing. And Kate, who planned only a quick
solitary walk – a breath of open air – falls and badly injures
herself. What began as a furtive walk has turned into a
mountain rescue operation . . .

Unbearably suspenseful, witty and wise, *The Fell* asks probing
questions about the place the world has become since
March 2020, and the place it was before. Sarah Moss's novel is
a story about compassion and kindness and what we must do
to survive, and it will move you to tears.

'One of the best writers at work in Britain today'
Fiona Mozley, author of *Elmet*

'Moss's star is firmly in the ascendant' *Guardian*

'The most brilliant writer. She deserves to win all the prizes'
Joanna Trollope

'One of our very best contemporary novelists' *Independent*